Very Kinky Girls

By

Mistress Elena Hexthorn

About the Book

Very Kinky Girls is a collection short extremely kinky stories. It is a debut sampler of seven tales of erotic wildness. Each girl embraces all aspects of their own explicit fantasies in each tale, whilst cloaked in the anonymity of London. Some girls are very gothic and dominant. Others are aroused by their submissive desires as they surrender to the will of a trusted confederate, which could be either male, female or both. The girls' tastes are very refined and often humorous. Their personalities are highly tuned towards deeply empowered psychological scenarios that satisfy a whole host of their own libertine and outrageous desires for their own private, lascivious entertainment.

About the Author

Mistress Elena Hexthorn is a real-life Mistress who has been running chambers and fetish clubs in London since the early 1990's, including the long-standing fetish event: London Fetish Fair. Trained in screen writing, short story writing and a keen photographer and painter. Many of the stories in the book are drawn from real life experiences in the world of fetish fantasy. This book is a precursor to her forthcoming debut novel "How to make Ghosts".

Contents

Very Kinky Girls

Elena Hexthorn

This edition published 2016

SEXT ME

Ellen sped towards St. Pancras station in London on her journey back from Manchester. She had had a lot of fun clubbing in the city, but decided she would also enjoy cultivating a little more fun on the train back home by picking out a stranger to flirt with. She enjoyed the way he looked at her as she crossed her legs high to surreptitiously show him her black lace stocking tops. Playfully, she leant over to stroke her 'tired' ankles. She could see that he was transfixed by the shine of her black patent spiked heels. It was the last train that night. Ellen always knew how best to take advantage of the final segment of an otherwise dull train journey by finding someone anonymous to play with, which she enjoyed when she was in the right frame of mind. Most of the time, she *was* in the right frame of mind. Occasionally, she would ask herself what the attraction was of turning on a stranger. She concluded that it might be out of boredom, or simply because she could. But in truth, she was just curious about what made the world tick outside of the bubble of her own private thoughts.

The last few passengers that had boarded the train at the previous stop had already taken their seats in another carriage. She was now alone in one of the cars apart from one suitably innocent looking young man who had been in the same carriage as her for some time. She made an educated guess that he had probably missed his stop so he could carry on observing her. It was a regular occurrence for her. She liked the look of this man. It took Ellen almost no time whatsoever to negotiate with the stranger to the get him to agree to go down on his knees in front of her on the carriage floor. She quietly guided his head between her legs so they could both enjoy the last few minutes of travel before the train pulled into St. Pancras Station. Ellen discovered quite some time ago that most men (given the opportunity for a little extracurricular smuttiness) would happily oblige to even the most spontaneous of her wishes. There wasn't a lot to say about the stranger. He was swarthy but was boyishly good looking. To Ellen's sensibilities, she felt that he was relatively attractive enough to warrant a quick session of oral, but nothing beyond that. She knew that it would be a quick hit of excitement for them both.

The train pulled in to the station. Ellen picked up her travel case and headed towards the exit door. The man followed behind her timidly.

'Can I come home with you?' he asked. His seemed very shy in asking her.

'I'd love you to,' she replied. 'But I don't think my husband would appreciate it very much,' she lied. She said that, because she didn't want him to feel rejected, but at the same point she was looking forward to going home and getting into a hot bath, more than anything else.

She started to walk away from him towards the station entrance, leaving the man standing on the platform. His face was a mixture of lust and excitement that had gone adrift. She shot him a huge grin and waved as she walked away. Sometimes, less was more. Had she carried on longer with him that it would have killed the fantasy. She preferred to enjoy leaving those images of the station in her mind to savour for the next time she decided to take the train.

As she stood in the queue for a taxi, she noticed that a series of texts began to pop up on her phone. She stared at the screen and decided that there must have been a drop-out in the mobile phone service whilst she had been in transit. She remembered that the tree-laden part of the countryside approaching London night had served to cut off her service before.

The first text she read was surreal. It said:

'Miss Ellen, I saw you at your last club. I think your face is banging. Gorgeous face. It really turned me on. I have been fantasizing about me sitting down then watching as you walk over to me. You bend over and pull up your skirt, forcing me to worship your ass. All I can think about is you sitting on me whilst rubbing your arse and pussy over my face. I can't get the image out of my head. It's driving me insane.'

The second text was even more intriguing:

'How do you feel about spitting in my mouth?' it read. The following text was even more bold. 'I think you are sexy as fuck and I just want you to hold my head back and piss in my mouth.'

A lot of people might see a text like that as abusive. But Ellen's inner curiosity and years of working in S&M clubs had taught her not to be so hasty without finding out a little bit more about the person that was sending the anonymous texts. Strangers had a way of opening to her. She enjoyed it. She felt that if they could keep it together enough to stay polite, (dirty but polite) they would warrant holding her attention. Once they crossed a line that made them seem less flirtatious and sexy in favour of sounding more disjointed and scary, she would delete the texts and vanish. But at first, it could be like a game of chicken between both parties to see how much of their fantasies they could put out there. For some people, this type of communication would be something that would never make it outside of their fantasies. But some of the texters really meant what they said, and given the right kind of permission would act on their desires. Over the course of her life, Ellen had found out a lot about the insides of men's minds this way, and saw that many of them had another side that seemed like a type of unopened flower. Most of them had the strangest vistas and spikes hiding away of inside the landscape of their minds. She wanted access to that. Finding out their innermost sexual cravings could be as addictive as opening a whole box of fortune cookies. However, some of those cookies just happened to taste more delicious than the others.

Either way, every kinky intelligent mind was potentially a new playground for her. She especially enjoyed finding out the extent of their fantasies and how far they had pursued them into reality. Ellen had a voracious appetite for exploring the inside of other people's minds. There was always something to learn from this. Running a fetish club over the years and publishing her contact number on nearly a million flyers made her used to getting a wide and varied cross section of phone messages and unusual text requests over that time. Also, being in that position had led her to decide to relax and enjoy these messages when they came to her. She also felt comforted in the knowledge that there were plenty of covertly kinky people in the world, hungry for new, yet-to-be specified pursuits in pleasure. If it was on her terms and they were respectful, a lot of interesting things could and would happen. It may sound strange, but it didn't really matter to her who they were in life or really, what they even looked like. What she was passionate about was the act of getting turned on, coupled with access to their dirty thoughts to keep her interested in her day. She loved it. The experience of intelligence and imagination was her primary directive. She loved the way she would sometimes get dirty texts from strangers designed to shock her, only to come back to them with something much worse. This was a type of game that she found challenging, and it could break up an otherwise dull day.

There was a certain impish look about Ellen's face. It was framed by the severe straight red fringe accompanied by her long, bobbed, ebony black hair. She always had a look in her eyes which was a mixture of vulnerability and ultra-coolness. Her face was difficult to define without taking a longer look. But in truth, it masked a mind that was constantly trying to calculate the next kinky escapade she could dream up to make life that bit more interesting. After much deliberation over the previous text, she managed to channel her inner rudeness to think of the dirtiest thing she could text back to the stranger.

'I have no problem spitting in your mouth. As I see it, it's still not as filthy as the state of the sheets that your Dad left my bed in last night.' Ellen laughed out loud as she typed. She hopped in the taxi that would ferry her back to her little flat in North London. She carried on typing another text to the stranger with some amusement.

'There's nothing I would like better than to hold you down with my arse on your face and force you to find out how far you can stick your tongue up my ass, if you think you're brave enough. Or is this all just a phone wank? And call me Mistress, you little cock fondler!' Ellen mashed her response fervently into the keypad.

'Yes Mistress,' he replied. 'I would so love to stick my tongue in your ass.'

'Well good,' replied Ellen. 'Send me a picture of your cock and your face. I want to see what I might be sitting on later.' Ellen typed the words quickly into the keypad of the telephone. She put the phone back in her bag to look at the London sights as they flashed past her on her way home.

The taxi arrived outside her flats. She dawdled up the path, searching for her keys. She could hear a series of texts buzzing through in her bag as she walked along.

'He seems keen,' she thought. 'I wonder which one it was from the last club?'

She searched her memory but came up with nothing. She thought about the last time she had been out, dressed head-to-toe in a maroon latex catsuit. It had been unzipped enough to show off a distracting display of cleavage. She remembered coolly chatting to a few people but so many seemed to be staring either at her the sleekness of her shiny catsuit or her cleavage. She didn't remember talking to that many new people. Her strongest recollection of the last event were the droves of different latex and leather clad club-goers, as they congregated along the seating and tables at the edge of the darkened club. She also recalled that she had spent a lot of time playing rubber nurse with two or three of the regular slaves at another club she had recently attended. She did remember attracting a bit of an audience at the time. But no one had approached her and offered anything remotely like the texts she was presently receiving. If she had, she may well have considered an offer at the time, provided she had liked the look of them.

Ellen opened her flat with a set of keys accented by a black leather mini crop. She put her travel case down and kicked off her shoes. She changed into a light blue and black baby doll nightgown, black stockings and fluffy high-heeled mules. Dressing up was her way of relaxing. She tied her hair up into a bunch on top of her head and started to think about a drinking a nice glass of prosecco in the bath. She cast an eye over the row of six-inch high-heeled shoes she had racked up above her four-poster bed.

'I wish someone would invent waterproof heels,' she mused. 'No one seems to have picked up that the high heel experience is truly incomplete until you can wear your high heels in the bath.' She walked to the cupboard and opened a large cardboard box containing a pair of black rubber thigh boots.

'I guess I could wear these as long as I don't get the soles wet,' she thought to herself.

She drew a bath, poured a glass of wine and put the boots on a small carved wooden table beside the tub. She retrieved her mobile phone from her hand bag and ferried it into the bathroom. She undressed and immersed herself in the hot bubbles, inhaling the scent of her almond soap as the steaming hot water gushed from the tap. As the bath filled, she carefully swung her legs over the side of the bath to dress herself in her latex boots. Having laced them into place, she rested them on the bath taps. She took a picture of them with her camera phone and admired the results. They looked good, she thought.

She looked at her phone to read her texts. There were two unread messages. Both were pictures. She downloaded them and perused the images with a spry look. The first picture was of a cock. It was average sized but quite thick and circumcised. The picture had been taken from above, but from what she could work out it wasn't an entirely unattractive looking appendage.

'Hmm, this might be promising,' she thought. 'It's still hard to tell from that angle.'

She continued to retrieve the next picture only to find a good looking male face with bright blue eyes. In the photograph, the young man was sitting at a table outside a café by a train station.

'He is hot,' she thought. 'Perhaps that is a face I could sit on.'

Ellen typed into the keypad again. 'You *are* hot. Is that really you? Because I wouldn't need much convincing to fuck you right now, if it is,' she texted. She capped it off with a second text attaching a picture of her boots resting just above the bubble bath. 'If you were here right now, I would have no problem getting you in this bathtub and holding you down. I would make you drink my piss until you were choking for air.'

A text quickly came back.

'Can I call?' it read.

'Yes,' replied Ellen. 'Give me one minute, then call.'

Ellen raised her pussy out of the water and took a picture of it on her phone. She then took another one of her pussy with her lips parted using her fingers to get a close-up view of her clit. Then, looking up into the camera, she took a final picture of her face and tits in the bubble bath and waited for the phone to ring. Of course, it did.

'Hello Mistress...' said a timid male voice on the other end of the line.

'Hello,' replied Ellen. '.. And who do I have the pleasure of speaking to this evening?'

'My name is David. I saw you at the last fetish club you ran. I was bowled over by you.'

'Well, thanks very much David, that's nice of you to say,' she returned politely. 'Now what are we going to do about these shameful texts you have been sending all evening? Are you playing with yourself?'

'Yes, I am, Mistress,' the timid voice replied.

'Well hang on then. I am going to send you a couple of pictures...' she said.

Ellen composed a text comprising of the pictures of herself naked in the bath. A text came back

'When were those taken, Miss?' was the reply.

'Right now. This is what I am doing,' she answered.

There was a moments silence...

'Call me back, slut,' she ordered.

The phone rang again.

'Now this chatting and texting is all very good but it's not going to satisfy me,' she said pointedly. 'How soon can you get to North London?'

'Well, I am about thirty minutes away.'

'Fine,' she said, smiling. 'I am going to text you my address and I expect you to be here in forty minutes, if you've got the nerve. If you don't have the nerve. Don't contact me again. Those are my terms.'

'Yes, Mistress. Yes, I do have the nerve, Mistress. I will be there,' said David.

'Good? How old are you by the way? I will see you in forty minutes, and incidentally if you aren't who you say you are in the photographs then don't bother coming. I value honesty above everything else. In fifty minutes, I won't answer the door. I think you might want to get moving.'

'Yes Mistress, the picture I sent is me. I'm twenty-six years old. I will leave right now.'

'Good,' she said 'And don't chicken out. I hate that.'

With that, she put down the phone and waited, sipping wine.

'Well this is going to make the evening interesting,' she thought to herself. 'Let's see if he's got the balls. Then let's see his balls,' she said to herself with a little laugh.

According to her phone, thirty-two minutes had passed when she heard her door bell ring. She was pleased about his decision to move quickly. So many men were happy to live in their heads. It was a rare breed that would take a risk. She found that an instant turn-on. She swung her high-heeled boots over the side of the bath, so that she could get out and answer the door. Donning a black satin robe, she walked to the front door. A young, shy, good-looking man entered the hallway. She ushered him in and shut the door behind him. He stood looking at her awkwardly in the tiny hall. She looked him up and down with a pleased look on her face. She had no recollection of him from any clubs that she may have been to recently. She parted her black satin robe to show him her naked body framed by her wet, thigh-length latex boots.

'On your knees, boy,' she demanded.

The man dropped to his knees in the hallway. She knew they would be more comfortable in the lounge or bedroom, but she loved the psychology of not letting him get more than a foot in the door before he had to assume a submissive role.

'Lick,' she ordered, pointing to the tip of her boot.

The man immediately dropped to his knees. Ellen threw her robe to the floor. She could feel the hardness of his tongue as it licked the lowest point of her rubber boot and worked its way up to the tops of the thighs. That was one of her ultimate erogenous zones: the top of her thighs. If someone had the presence of mind to work out that kissing and licking her thighs attentively was enough to drive her crazy, she would be all over them like a starving artist. She turned around and ordered him to kiss the backs of her thighs. She then pushed her hands against the wall. The pleasure and the sensations he was causing made her feel as though it would have been a good opportunity to fuck the stranger there and then in the hallway, but she didn't want it all to be over so soon.

Unabashedly, 'Ellen parted her arse cheeks and guided his head towards her ass.

'I want you to stick your tongue as far up my ass as it will go. And I want to be impressed by your efforts as well,' she said with a sly smile. What she loved about this scenario was the lighted front of the frosted glass door in the hallway. There was more than enough visibility in the doorway so that any passer by outside would be able to pick out the naked form of a woman in long black boots being serviced by another figure on their knees. It always excited her to think someone might catch a quick glimpse and be shocked.

'Before you do that, go into the living room and strip for me. I want to watch you dance.' She grabbed his hand and led him into her living room. She leant over to her computer and put some music on. For her own black humour, she had chosen Q-Lazzarus's "Goodbye Horses". She knew by his age he probably wouldn't get the joke. But she did.

The music pumped out from the speakers on the wall. She flopped down into a zebra print low chair and crossed her rubber clad boots, waiting for her new subject to dance for her.

'Come on,' she said. 'You're amongst friends, and you know it's going to turn me on if you do it,' she said, egging him on. She slid one hand along her neck, down one breast and along her belly. Her hand finally rested on her pussy. 'If you want to get in here,' she said looking at him seriously, 'I'm going to need a little show from you. It's what I require.'

Self-consciously the man began to take his shirt off. She gazed across his toned body and tattoos and slipped a finger into her cunt as she watched. He sat on the floor and removed his boots in an unceremonious manner. He then attempted his highly embarrassed dance for her. She watched and waited until he was stripped down to his boxer shorts. At that point, she halted him from removing them.

Alighting from her chair, she slowly crawled over to where he was dancing, in time to the music. Kneeling before him, she roughly ripped his boxer shorts down to watch his cock spring upwards like a toy. She grabbed it and licked the base of his prick.

'That was a nice dance, David. I like it when a man is compliant,' she said. The next thing she did was something that he wasn't expecting. She engulfed the entire length of his cock into her mouth. Removing it, she looked up at him with her two big, round eyes.

'Force it. Force-feed your cock to me,' she ordered, opening her mouth wide.

The man grabbed the base of his cock and guided it into her mouth. Her warm, wet pink lips encircled it fully. She reached forward to try and get the entire length of his cock as far into the back of her throat as she could. She gagged a little bit and choked. She felt close to the edge of vomiting but held her mind together so she could practice one of her favourite fetishes: deep throating. Tears streamed out of her eyes and the residue of her black eye make-up ran down her cheeks. She got into a steady rhythm, choking and thrusting her head up and down his shaft. He groaned loudly at the sight and feeling of her forceful sucking.

'Mistress I am going to cum,' he groaned.

Ellen immediately pulled her mouth away from his cock and grabbed the head of his prick between her two fingers, scrunching it hard.

'Oh no you're not,' she said with an evil smile. 'Not yet you're not. You're going to attend to me first.'

Standing up, she put her hand on his shoulder and forced him down on his knees.

'Get on all fours for me, you dirty slut,' she said.

Ellen also got onto all fours herself and backed her ass up into his face.

'You haven't finished licking me yet,' she retorted. 'Concentrate on sucking my pussy this time. I want to see how much you can please my clit. Make sure you lick nice and hard.' Ellen felt a rush of pleasure as David furiously licked her pussy and asshole. She pushed her booted leg back to caress his cock with her foot.

'Good boy...' she hissed. 'Now bite my pussy lips,' she said. 'I like that.'

David did as he was ordered. Ellen could feel a rising pleasure in her that was making her begin to feel an aching to be fucked. Not being able to stand much more. She rolled over and parted her legs.

'Come on, fuck me, do as your told. Fuck me nice and hard,' she said.

Ellen raised her ass up high, sticking her pussy right into David's face. With one last suck of her pussy lips, he plunged the entirety of his cock sharply into her cunt. The friction of his fat prick against her pussy made her moan with pleasure. A 'pop' of air escaped and she swung one her latex boots over his neck, digging her heel into his back.

'You are a fucking slut!' she said forcefully, in between pumps. 'Now, make me cum!' she demanded.

She looked up as the young tattooed man as he laboured in earnest. She could see that he was trying to fuck her as hard as she had directed him to. She let out a sigh as the rush of a rising orgasm began to build inside her cunt. He slowed down, carefully teasing her, dipping his cock in and out of her pussy. Frustrated, she could take no more and wrapped both of her boots round his back, digging her heels into his ass.

'Fuck me like your life depended on it!' she demanded. Ellen shut her eyes and held her breath. The force of her orgasm washed over her and she let out a hard scream. Her patience had waned. It was too much to bear for another moment. She rolled over onto her side, post orgasm and stuck her ass in his face.

'Mistress, I have not cum yet.' he said breathing heavily.

'Oh, you will. But we have a little more playing to do before that happens,' she stated. She sighed heavily with satisfaction. 'I expect to get a few more orgasms out of you first. I think you are a fun thing to play with. I am in no hurry to stop.'

Standing up, she led him into the bathroom and sat him on the glass seat on her toilet. She ordered him to kiss her again then filled the bath with more hot water. She stopped him momentarily and ordered him to hold his head back and open his mouth. Slowly, she let a stretched line of spit drip onto his tongue. She watched as his cock sprung hard to attention.

'That's hot,' he whispered as he looked up at her.

'Good, now lie down in the bath,' she said. There was a tone of insistence in her voice that he could not resist.

David lifted himself carefully into the bath and got into position. His body was immersed in the warm water. He watched as Ellen precariously straddled the sides of the bath tub in her black rubber boots and stood over him. She grabbed onto the rail holding up the shower curtain to steady herself.

'Open your mouth, dirty whore,' she said. 'It's time for target practice.'

David lay expectantly in the bath. He grabbed his swollen cock and started playing with it. He opened his mouth and waited, with a feeling of trepidation. Ellen edged herself closer to his mouth and squatted over it. After a short pause, a hard stream of hot piss gushed out of her pussy into his mouth. He gurgled and choked as it ran over of the sides of his face.

'Shut your eyes,' she said. Carefully she manoeuvred her pussy over his face and let another stream of sharp piss unleash into his mouth. 'Now swallow,' she said.

'Mistress,' I can hardly breathe!'

Ellen lifted herself up, away from his mouth and turned around to survey the situation he was protesting about.

'You look okay to me. Don't worry. Although, oxygen is a very valuable commodity in this domicile. I don't think you can drown this way. It certainly wasn't the case the last time I checked, anyway,' she said disaffectedly. 'Wait there, and keep your eyes shut,' she added.

Leaving the room momentarily, she returned with a pair of prison handcuffs and a black blindfold. These items were things from her collection that she had amassed from her years of running S&M clubs.

On her return, she raised him up out of the bath. He was now in a standing position. She handcuffed his hands to the top of the shower and tightly tied the blindfold around his eyes.

'Now I've got you,' she said. She let out a playful, evil laugh.

She pulled the plug, letting the water out of the bathtub. She stood in the bath behind him. Lightly, she dragged her nails up and down the length of his chest and thighs. She lifted the shower hose and turned it to the 'cold' position. In short bursts, she aimed the head of the shower at first his back, then his lower torso and lastly right towards the centre of his asshole.

David let out a little scream.

'There, there David. Ellen will make it better,' she soothed. She parted his arse cheeks and stuck her tongue firmly up his ass. Reaching again, she grabbed his cock and began to play with it.

David was dumbstruck and silent. Quietly, she un-cuffed him and made him face her.

'Pick me up and fuck me,' she said climbing onto his sturdy frame.

David did as was ordered. Ellen delighted in the feeling of his cock darting in and out of her pussy as he bore the weight of her on his powerful body. With David still blindfolded, she could feel his senses sharpen, as he concentrated on fucking her in time to her moans. Ellen bounced up and down on the girth of his cock. He felt like a fairground ride. She threw her head back and disappeared into a part of her mind that forgot the rest of the world outside. All she could see in her mind was wave after wave of black searing pleasure and stars. They came hurtling towards her in a stream of what felt like tiny explosions. For a moment, she forgot everything that was going on around her and focussed on the centre of the stars. They seemed to send endless messages to her pussy telling her that all she needed to do was cum. Another orgasm started to rise inside of her. But she began to feel a deviant aching to have his cock inside of her ass before that could happen.

'Carry me to the bed,' she demanded.

'I can't see Mistress,' he replied with a confused tone.

Ellen whipped off his blindfold and looked at him pointedly.

'Now!' she ordered.

With his cock still impaled on her pussy he hobbled to the next room. Ellen looked at his face, smiling at his efforts.

'I want you to dip your cock in my ass before I cum again,' she said. David didn't need any convincing as he guided the thickness of his cock carefully into her arse. It took about a minute to force the head of his penis past her tight arse hole, but she soon opened and enjoyed the sensation as she forced herself backwards to take the full length of his shaft. He grabbed her ass and made the first thrust really count.

'Aagh!' she screamed. 'Yes! Get your fucking cock up my ass you dirty slut. I can't believe you'd come over and within an hour be fucking a total stranger in the ass. You are such a dirty whore! You should be ashamed of yourself. Now fuck me and make me cum you fucking whore!' she shouted with excitement. The dark feeling of having a submissives strange cock thrusting into her ass filled her with a deep glow of perverted satisfaction within her. She pictured herself from another point in the room, kneeling on all fours on the bed in black rubber boots with this young stranger sticking it to her. She craned her neck round to watch him grab her ass and thrust harder into her. Suddenly another desire came into her mind.

'Stop!' she ordered.

Looking a little confused, he *eventually* did.

'Lie down on the bed', she directed. Grabbing a pair of arm and leg restraints from a nearby case, she laced him up into the leather garments. She then restrained him, spread eagled onto the bed and let out a huge sigh.

'You look so fucking good like that,' she said in a soft tone.

She looked down at his cock and gave it a playful smack.

'Your cock has been very bad tonight. It will have to be punished for all its' crimes.'

'Mistress, I was only following orders,' he said defensively.

'That's neither here nor there,' she said. Her voice had a demonic joviality in it. 'Your cock has to know that, for every action there is a reaction, and that there is no true appreciation of pleasure without a little pain to compliment it.'

From a case beside the bed, she produced a set of black clothes pegs. She began to attach them in perfect order along the length of his cock. Carefully, she pinched up the skin on his shaft as she attached them one by one. She had managed to attach 23 in total to his cock and balls. She looked down at him with an icy stare.

'Now you have a choice. You can either let me whip the pegs off your cock one by one as you count, or you can let me suffocate you with my pussy for three times as many seconds. It's up to you,' she said. Her face was devilish as she looked over him and savoured his predicament.

David paused for a moment. She could see the clockwork of his decisions moving through of his mind by the look in his eyes. He knew that by either path he chose, there would be an ordeal to face. And previously, by the way he had felt overwhelmed from the hot gulps of piss he had been drinking that had nearly choked him; she was pretty sure he was going to choose the whipping.

'Mistress, I have never had my cock whipped before, and I am a bit frightened,' he said.

'Well,' she replied. 'There's a first time for everything. So, what's it to be?'

'I think, erm, suffocate me with your pussy...' he said. She could hear the relenting sound of his answer as he chose what seemed to her, like the easier option.

'So be it!' she said, with a glint in her eye. Quickly she crawled up to the top of the bed and firmly lowered herself onto his restrained body, planting her pussy on his face. At first, he seemed very keen on the whole idea. He sucked and bit at her pussy lips. And that started to make her feel hot all over again. Being very sly, she reversed away from him and grabbed a short black leather cat o' nine tails that she kept hidden on a lower shelf beside her bed. David, engrossed in his licking and sucking couldn't see what was coming next, but it certainly wasn't going to be him.

Carefully, Ellen raised her arm to steady it. Aiming straight and true, she lashed a firm swipe across his cock to unsnap the first of the clothes peg away from his cock.

'Oww!' he screamed, suddenly realising what she had just done.

Ellen let him up for air. 'You just be a good boy and concentrate on licking my pussy. Besides, that's all you're good for, you know I am right,' she quipped.

She raised her whipping arm again and sharply dislodged three pegs at once from the length of his erect cock. Somewhere near her pussy she could hear his muffled scream. The sound made her laugh sadistically.

'Good boy, well done! Only two more minutes to go!' she teased.

She varied the strength and timing as she whipped each peg away from his prick. The not knowing when the next blow would come made her slave hypersensitive. She tittered as his whole body jumped with each stroke of the whip. As the last few pegs succumbed to the stings of her weapon, she reattached them with her mouth. Licking along the shaft of his red raw cock, she pulled the pegs away, painstakingly trying to pinch the skin and perpetuate the slowest of torments.

As the last peg was removed, she hit the fourth minute. It was a longer amount of time than she had contracted with him. She raised her ass from his face and turned around. She wanted to see whether he had *survived,* or not.

'You're a good slave, David. You have been good, now you can have a reward. So, now I am going to make you cum.'

'I don't know if I can after that Mistress,' he said. His sounded full of exhaustion.

'You'll do as your told, boyee,' she replied curtly.

Ellen unshackled him and used some spare rope already attached to the uprights of the bed to tie him across the frame of her four-poster.

'And you look good in that position, too,' she mused.

'Now for my last trick, I am going to make you cum in that position,' she said to David. She knelt to the floor and licked the base of his toes, working her way up his legs and resting at the inside of his thighs. She stood up and roughly grabbed his pectoral muscles and sucked at his nipples. From behind the bed, she reached over and threw both bedroom windows open. A rush of freezing air billowed in from the night outside. She knelt before him and gently put his cock between her teeth. Carefully, she pulled the skin of his cock and let it run along the white porcelain of her teeth. Her wet lips slid over his cock, gently caressing it with her mouth.

'A... B... C... D...' she began to recite and she forced his cock into her throat. 'When we get to Z, I want you to give me all of your spunk.'

She continued, reciting letter after letter. She observed him as he looked down at her, watching as she sucked his cock. Ellen concluded that he was potentially going to find it hard to not cum before the letter Z. By the time she reached 'S' she could see that he was straining. She started to speed up. Again, she impaled her mouth on his cock, still making muffled letter sounds as she tried to get him to cum in time to her reciting of the alphabet. She stopped and looked at him straight in the eye.

'I want you to shoot your spunk into the back of my throat,' she whispered to him.

'W... X... Y... Z!' she announced. In a split second, she forced one of her fingers deep into his ass as he came. A hard pulse of his thick load shot heavily into the back of her throat.

'Aaargh! Oh my God! 'he screamed.

She looked up at him as his face strained. She opened her mouth and gargled with his cum. She then swallowed it.

'Yummy,' she said with a satisfied smile.

She untied him and he collapsed onto the bed. He curled up into the foetal position.

'Good boy,' she said. 'Good slave David. You were very good. You pleased me,' Ellen said smiling thoughtfully. Playfully, she snapped one of the handcuffs again onto his wrist and fixed it to the bed. David looked at her with a face of pure confusion. Ignoring his expression, she got up and mashed a new text into the keypad.

'Now, since you've been such a good boy and done everything I have asked you. I know my pretty friend Marta would enjoy the exact same servicing as well. So, you just lie down and relax. I think my friend will probably be round in about ... forty minutes,' she smiled. 'And, I am looking forward to watching another show.' Ellen let out a terribly sadistic giggle and left the room.

WOLVES

Lucy and Stephen sat-side-by side at a small metal table. Stephen pushed his thigh against Lucy's as he lit her cigarette. They both watched as people bustled past their table, which was planted on the pavement outside a busy London cafe. The broad, white-and-green striped canopy above the corner cafe dimmed the rays of the fading sunlight. Dusk began to pick out the neon signs in the Soho street. The gradually blazing neon gave the area such an exciting glow. It also induced a feeling for both of being somewhere meaningful. Soho had a way of attracting the city's most unusually beautiful moths and fireflies in human form. Lucy and Stephen could easily be described as two of those exotic creatures.

'What do you think of that one over there?' said Lucy, as she spied a young girl with pale pink hair. The girl was wearing a mini skirt and white fluffy jacket. She rushed past Lucy and Stephen on the opposite side of the street.

'Yeah,' said Stephen. 'I'd be up for that. But only as a snack. I think we should pick out the one we see with the most style in the next ten minutes. That's our first game for this evening. Let's find someone really interesting.'

'Okay,' said Lucy. 'Ten minutes, starting from now.'

Lucy stared up and down the road. She then grabbed Stephen at his shoulder and bit his cheek passionately.

'This game is easy,' she said. 'You have the most style.'

The hairs on the back of Stephen's arm stood up.

'I don't know how you always manage to do that,' he said.

'Do what?' she laughed.

'Make the hairs stand up on the back of my arm. Still, after all this time, you have the same effect on me.'

'That's not the only thing I plan to make stand up today,' she quipped flirtatiously.

The couple carried on watching as a vast selection of anonymous people briskly filed past. Businessmen in grey suits with black briefcases strode along the street purposefully, only to then quietly slip into the seedy doorways of massage parlours marked 'model upstairs'. And if they weren't doing that they would alternately be sliding into one of the adult book stores by nipping through their slatted, primary-coloured plastic curtains. Elderly American tourists stared at random buildings in the street looking lost and conspicuous in their brightly coloured rain wear. Huge gangs of students in matching windcheaters trundled along the cobbles of the street speaking in animated foreign tones. But the regular working denizens of Soho were usually much more quiet and unassuming. They were barely noticeable as they went about their business in the district. Very few of the varied cast of visitors to Soho noticed the unusually dressed Lucy and Stephen as the two coiled their legs around each other at the pavement cafe table. They both gazed above themselves to survey the flurry of passers-by. London was often too busy to notice the details. Stephen ran his hand along Lucy's leg then rested it discreetly between her thighs.

'I like how the odd person here and there is noticing that I have my hand between your legs but won't say anything about it,' Stephen said, with a satisfied smile. Lucy raised one eyebrow at him and lowered one of her eyelids. She smiled back.

Lucy ran her hand along his arm and turned towards him. She grabbed the underside of his knee with one hand and let her long black hair spill onto his shoulder, as she licked his neck.

'I like a little bit of showing off too,' she whispered.

Despite the mechanised comings and goings of the local populace, they both knew that the level of public display they were putting on was still enough to draw a few disapproving frowns, even in this extremely liberal minded part of the city. Tourists were usually the first people to gawk. But Lucy liked it. So too, did Stephen. Because, in truth, they both really didn't care that much what anyone thought. They didn't have to. The would never see these people again. That was the beauty of living in a megacity.

'When you do that Stephen...' said Lucy. 'I feel as though I want to hold you down and have you right here. I feel like I want to eat you a-fucking-live.'

'Well,' said Stephen. 'It's no fun if you go straight to devourment right away, you know. Not when I can tease the fuck out of you first.'

Stephen discreetly slipped his finger under the band of her black lace knickers and let it rest inside her pussy. His explorations found her cunt to be soaking wet.

Lucy tossed her head back with torment. Her hair spilled down over her grey silk velvet coat and she gasped with alarm. She closed her eyes and subtly parted her legs. Her girlish face held an innocence that masked an ocean of dirty whims, all of which were still trapped inside of her mind. Behind her virginal look, there was a calculating brain. It was a brain that was constantly planning every debauched fantasy that she wanted to experience right now, and then next with her lover.

Still, in that little side street, no one could tell what interactions were going on between the two. People would only have been able to truly tell what was going on between them if they were to stop and closely study them. That was the only way to build up the real picture of their current interactions. But thankfully, London was just too polite a city to complain about the kind of people Lucy and Stephen were. And so often the hustle of downtown life had a way of concealing a thousand curious incidents at once. He lifted his other hand and ran it across the décolletage of Lucy's neck. He whispered in her ear.

'You look pretty today,' he said. 'I wonder how many men have walked past and looked at you, wanting to fuck you. Men, and women as well.'

Lucy hid her face in the crook of Stephen's neck. The lascivious way he had uttered that missive in her ear had driven her to a point of lust that bordered on madness. He had a skill for getting into Lucy's mind and under her skin. Stephen was always elegantly dressed in black with a carefully chosen accent of vintage eccentricity that she found very sexy. To her, his presence had a sexual charge that just made her feel like she wanted to do whatever he told her to, especially as almost everything he told her to do was designed to get her off. She could feel herself getting wet as Stephen discreetly shoved his finger deeply inside of her pussy, and covered his actions with the skirt of her coat.

'You like that don't you?' he said.

Lucy blushed and her voice wavered. 'Oh, fuck yes, I do. I don't know how much longer I am going to last, out here like this,' she said unsteadily. She could feel the slow torment of Stephen's afternoon teasing starting to take its' toll. The fireworks of lust in her mind began to harangue her for sexual release. She could feel herself wildly starting to entertain the thought of what the actual consequences of ripping Stephen's clothes off and mounting him right there in the street might be. She suspected that he might insist she refrain from doing that so publicly, but she was nearing the point mentally, of throwing all the rules out of the window. She knew they were at her favourite café. She also knew *he would* eventually forgive her for her indiscretion of ravishing him on the spot. But the bit she wouldn't be so happy about would be the loss of their favourite spying location in the centre of town. She knew they would get banned from the café if she undertook a course of public sex at dinner time. She resolved to relent and let Stephen continue to have the upper hand with his covert finger fucking. Lucy rocked backwards and forwards, discreetly trying to gain more purchase from Stephen's dexterous fingers.

'I think you should finish your coffee so we can go,' said Stephen.

'I agree.' she said. 'If we don't go soon, I am going to get arrested for public indecency and causing an affray. But with that said, you have wound me up this afternoon so much that I am far beyond caring about the consequences. I think it will be you that should get arrested for misbehaving and not me.

'Well, I think we would both get into trouble,' said Stephen.

'Want to find out?' said Lucy.

Stephen took another cigarette from his black leather cigarette case. He lit it. He turned and smiled at Lucy as he put his cigarette in the ashtray. With one hand, he grabbed her by her hair and pulled her towards his lips to kiss her. With the other hand, he shoved his finger right up into her pussy. Lucy winced. A column of desire raced up and down the length of her body making her feel dizzy. Because, despite his spidery, foppish elegance; Stephen was all male. The way he could pull her towards him and carefully manipulate her next thought or feeling was something she found intoxicating and addictive. He always had the most amazing scent on, as well. It was a sharp aroma of cedar wood and musk, with an undertone of jasmine and myrrh. The scent was very masculine, but faintly sweet. Every time she was near to him in his orbit, she was quickly sucked in and mesmerised by his presence. He had this magnetism that made her feel like she wanted to crawl inside of his mind and never come out again. His mind was warm and sexual. It made her feel like a star being swallowed by a black hole. In the same sense, when she was away from him, it made her feel like she had broken a bit of science and the natural laws of the universe. There was nothing right in her world when that happened. Her personal productivity and interest in life would wane into a sharp decline. When she was away from him, she felt so much less alive, especially because the games stopped. Without him, she felt herself to be trundling through a waste ground of identical zombies in the city. What she was most addicted to was the way his playfulness made her imagination dance. It was engrossing. He always left her aching for another hit.

Stephen stood up and put out his hand for her. With a short, silver-spiked black leather glove, she accepted.

'I don't think we are going to find anyone suitable today, this way. I think it's time we departed,' said Stephen.

The flowing skirt of her full-length coat swished gracefully behind her and she walked up to the next corner of the road. She stopped and turned to see Stephen standing several paces behind her.

'I was just watching how you walk,' he said.

She put her hand out to grab his. They walked along the road together. Her lower torso began to shake. She found herself physically overwhelmed by the slow burning lust he had instilled in her, after the hours of teasing he had put her through in that public place. She spied an alleyway and decided to take a risk. She him by the hand into the tiny side street. She pushed him up against the wall. Commandeering the situation for a moment, she dragged him further into a darkened alcove in the side-street. She knelt in front of him in the fading light.

'I can't take it anymore. I've just got to...' Lucy unzipped Stephen's trousers. She quickly impaled her glossy red lips on the head of his cock. He gasped as he felt her mouth work its way to the very base of his prick. Stephen looked down with pleasure watching the spectacle of her lips encircling his hardness. He threw his head back, feeling almost drunk as he listened to the delicious noises of her slurping on the shaft of his penis. Stephen moaned.

'Are you going to cum for me, Daddy?' Lucy said in a soft, high-pitched girly voice. The voice she affected by far preceded her twenty-five years, but she used it because she knew a squeaky girlie voice always turned him on. 'Please Daddy, fill up my mouth. I'm so hungry for you,' she squeaked.

Two pairs of footsteps entered the alleyway, belonging to some strangers passing by. Stephen and Lucy stopped to listen as their footfalls got closer to them. Stephen suffered a moment of anxiety over the thought of being discovered, yet at the same time he also felt an immense surge of pleasure. Another part of his mind delighted with the idea of being observed by strangers as his beautiful girl sucked greedily on his prick. It was only a minor dilemma about what to do about them. He wouldn't do anything. He waited until the footsteps got very close.

'I am going to cum for you, darling,' he said. 'Just as those two men are within five feet of us… then I am going to give you all of my cum.' He could barely believe what he was saying to her, but he also felt determined to try and focus on making it happen.

Lucy felt the same surge of excitement run through her veins. She felt both hands on her head as he grabbed it strongly and began to fuck her mouth. She could taste his salty pre- cum and male sweat mixed with the scent of his cedar wood scented cologne. Closing her eyes, she thought about the image of being discovered sucking Stephen's cock by the two strangers. Engaging in this kind of exhibitionism was always like an out-of-the-body experience for Lucy. Her mind lighted up thinking about the reality that she was part of a couple who were satisfying their pleasures in a dark, anonymous alleyway in London. The thought of it made her pussy feel ready to involuntarily squirt. She was overwhelmed with a mixture of excitement, shame, fear and uncontrollable lust. Stephen forced his cock harder into the back of her throat with more strongly-paced strokes. She looked up at him with wide eyes, feeling a desperate urge to sexually please him, but also please herself with the taste of his cum. The strangers' footsteps got very close. The footfalls sounded heavy, like steel toe-capped boots often worn by workmen. Stephen forced his cock into her mouth with greater speed and intensity as she heard the fateful noise of the two pairs of boots stop right beside them. Lucy stopped what she was doing. She looked up to see the smiling faces of two men in their early thirties. There was a momentary pause of thought that seemed like an aeon. All four stared at each other. Stephen looked down into Lucy's eyes with a gleaming grin. It was even larger than the ones the two strangers had been flashing at Lucy. A heavy surge of cum exploded into Lucy's mouth. Stephen shut his eyes and groaned. After a moment, Stephen made Lucy stand up. He spun her round and grabbed her upper arms. He held them behind her back as he displayed her to the two men. He kissed her neck from behind her and stared at them both squarely.

'Would you like to try?' he said.

Both glanced at each other and then made sideways glances up and down the darkened alley. It was easy for Lucy to tell by the looks on their faces that the answer to Stephen's question was "Yes". Stephen pulled her further back into the alcove and forced her to her knees again. He bent down to whisper in her ear.

'I want you to suck these two men off, now,' he said within earshot of the men. 'Show them what you can do.'

She looked up at him and nodded obediently. He pulled down her blouse and jacket at the shoulders and roughly pulled her tits out of her bra, displaying her naked frame to the two men.

'Tell them to touch your tits,' he whispered.

Lucy complied. It took all the strength she could garner to speak like that to the two strangers, she managed to force out the words. She still felt that she wanted to comply with Stephen's wishes.

'Please, will you play with my tits?' Lucy said the to the two men. Obligingly, the two men started to grab and fondle her breasts. She could see from the shapes in their trousers that their pricks were becoming rock hard. Her excitement increased as Stephen's re-hardening cock pressed itself firmly against her the back of her head and mingled with her hair. She moved her face closer towards the men's bulges and looked up at them hungrily. Her dirty mind again perfectly masked by her feigned look of expectant innocence. She brushed her hands gently across both men's crotches, and they began to unzip their pants. Soon, she felt the force of their two cocks pushing towards her face. She grabbed them, and began to stroke them. Hypnotically, they stared down at her as they fondled her breasts. One of the men, the younger one; had a large fat cock. The shaft of his penis was very wide and thick. Glistening beads of pre-cum were already dripping from the head. The second man's cock was more average, but when she went to touch it was amazed by how taut it was and the amount of blood that seemed to be pulsating through it. She began to rub them, up and down... they looked down at her and smiled, thrusting their hips forward until their pricks were nearly touching her face. Lucy looked up towards Stephen for approval. He smiled down at her and kissed her on the top of her head.

'Good girl,' he said. 'You are a very good girl. Now I want you to suck them for me,' he whispered.

Lucy winced again as the two men stepped a few inches closer towards her. Stephen looked down at her as he stood over her with his hands on her shoulders. He watched on with pleasure as she obeyed his orders to suck the two random men's cocks. She sucked, noting their unfamiliar flavours. Her tongue ran smoothly in turns along the shafts of the blood-engorged flesh of the two strangers. She alternated between wanking one as she sucked the other, then she would swap over. Every now and again she turned her eyes up again towards Stephen, still seeking his blessing. She would receive it from him as a pair of sparkling, laughing dark eyes. He rubbed his cock into her back and bent down to speak quietly in her ear yet again.

'You do know what you have to say now, don't you dear?' he said in a low tone.

Lucy did know. She knew because this, by far, wasn't the first time Stephen had conscripted her into one of his sexually dark plots.

'Yes' she replied softly to him. She turned to face the two men again. She took one cock in each hand and began to rhythmically rub them.

'Please give me your spunk,' she said. 'I want you to cum all over my face, on my tits and in my mouth. I just want you to rub your cocks all over me until I am covered in your cum,' she said with a little lilt of embarrassment in her speech.

The two men seemed happy to oblige her request. They stared down, transfixed at the girls' pert pink breasts as they continued to grab and fondle them, whilst she focussed on maintain the hardness of their cocks. She moaned again as she could feel the pressure of their spunk start to spurt. She jammed both into her mouth to ensure she would be able to get a double dose of the taste of their spunk. Neither of them was a disappointment. The first stranger thrust his head back as he took his cock in his hand and rubbed it hard across Lucy's lips. She shot his load with a hard spurt onto her tongue and down over her tits. The second man, with a loud grunt; forced his cock into her cheek for three or four more strokes. He stared down at her and grabbed one of her tits as hard as he could. His face strained as an ocean of cum dripped over her face. Most of it landed in her hair. Lucy wiped the cum off her face and ran the remainder of the spunk along her tongue. She swallowed it all.

'Thank you,' she said.

'And now for the main course,' said Stephen. He helped steady Lucy to her feet. With an unearthly force of physical strength, he grabbed one man by his arms and Lucy in turn grabbed the opposite stranger. Simultaneously they felt a surge of intense orgasmic pleasure as they bit down hard into the men's necks. Lucy could feel the life force drain out from the man and into her own body as she drank his blood. The satiation she felt was similar to the feeling of the beginning of an orgasm, but it was always an orgasm without release.

It was now pitch black in the alleyway. Cheap, underpowered lights from a closed nearby shop flickered on and off. The two silently adjusted their clothes and walked hand-in-hand out of the side street. Neither of them turned to look back at the two blood-drained bodies heaped on top of each other in the secluded alcove of the alleyway.

'I love you Stephen,' said Lucy. 'You have this way of making even the most unpleasant tasks seem like a party. You have made me what I am today, in more ways than one.'

'Well, they might be finished for the day... those two,' he said with a sinful lilt in his voice. 'but we're not. You still have more of my pleasures to attend to today my darling girl.'

'Oh?' she said with an inquisitorial tone. 'Is that so?'

'Oh yes,' he said, as they strode towards the underground train station. Stephen grabbed her hand tightly. Lucy put her arm around Stephen's waist and grabbed his ass with a hint of affectionate glee.

The pair entered the tube station and walked down the stairs.

'Are we going home?' she said.

'Yes, briefly,' he said. '... then, you'll see.'

They boarded the tube train. Lucy sat down on the only empty seat and looked up as Stephen stood above her protectively. Forgetting herself, she grabbed his leg by the back of his knee and rested her head against his thigh. Stephen carefully pushed her away so he could bend down briefly to speak to her, trying his best to make sure no one else could hear what he was saying on the noisy tube train.

'Bad girl, you can't do that right now ... I am extremely hard and if you do that again, everyone is going to know. So, you've got to be my good girl and not touch me like that for the moment,' he said to her with a very serious look.

Lucy crossed her legs and tensed the muscles of her pussy. She was still ridiculously turned on to the point of almost being in an altered state of consciousness. She felt very edgy in this situation. All day he had made her wait for an orgasm, and she was still nowhere near to getting it. She folded her arms and crossed her legs as she desperately tried not to make eye contact with Stephen, because he was the distracting object of her lust. Instead, she elected to focus on the least sexual looking person on the train. It was a kindly looking old woman with many bags of shopping propped up on her lap. She studied the patterns of the flowers on the woman's purple jacket to try and distract herself. It was the only thing she could think of trying to do, in order to stay obedient to her Master's will. The lady locked eye contact with her and winked. Looking back at her with a slight expression of surprise, she turned to study Stephen as he stood tall above her on the train. It was blatantly obvious that his hard cock was still straining through the cloth of his trousers within inches of her face. She felt her face turn red hot, as she blushed.

Thankfully they finally arrived at their tube stop. The two nipped speedily onto the lift that led them out of the station doors. Walking quickly, they headed back towards their North London flat.

The echoes of their steps resounded loudly and quickly along the pavement as they strolled past many grand, Victorian red brick houses until they reached their own residence. It was a Bauhaus-movement inspired building. "ISOKON" was written on the side of the beautiful architectural masterpiece in large silver letters in sleek, kitsch 1920's lettering. The clean, white minimalist lines of the building stood out unusually in the eye line of all the cottages and studios nearby. Lucy made to walk up the stairs to their front door, but Stephen pulled her back to him.

'Not that way darling, this way,' he said, walking her towards the building's garages.

Lucy followed him and watched as he produced the key to the garage and unlocked the door. He pulled up the garage door to reveal their immaculate, sleek black 1960's vintage jaguar. He pulled her into the darkness of the back of the car port and pulled on a chain in the ceiling that turned on a dimmed interior light. Glancing across the various tools and fixtures hanging on the wall, he lifted a roll of black gaffer tape.

'Strip, Lucy.' he ordered.

With eyes cast down, she obeyed. Lucy began to take off her clothes until she stood in front of him wearing just her black bra and knickers, and seamed hold-up stockings. He ripped a piece of tape from the roll and placed it across her mouth. With another rip, he bound her wrists tightly together and led her to the back of the car. He forced her to place her hands over the over the door of the car boot. He kicked her legs apart. Slowly, with his hot breath searing over her neck, she could feel as his fingers once again began to probe her flesh. He thrust his fingers roughly inside her pussy. She let out a muffled moan. The tease and torment of her cunt was back and she could feel her pussy lips begin to part hungrily, feeling the maddening intensity of aching for him to fuck her. His latest actions had made her need of him much worse. Lucy swayed dizzily. The consensual control was a massive turn on for her. The blood she had imbibed earlier, felt like it had drained entirely out of her head and was now concentrated into her cunt. She felt faint. Stephen unlocked the trunk of the car.

'You're going in there,' he said firmly. He bundled her into the boot of the car and slammed the door on top of her.

Inside, wrapped only in her black underwear, short black leather gloves and black gaffer tape, she squirmed helplessly as she felt the car begin to move off.

In the darkness, the beautiful black car rolled smoothly out of the garage. Stephen had left the bundle of Lucy's outer garments on a pile in the middle of the garage floor. Faintly, she could hear music emanating from the car's radio. She smiled to herself as she could hear Stephen singing along to "Nirvana's" song "Come as you are." It was always a comfort to her when she could feel him being in so much physical and psychological control of her. She felt completely under his power in every way. But he also made her feel entirely safe. This relationship had always been like an emotional contract between them. They both wanted it. But there were instances where she felt she wanted it more. She wanted it more than anything else on the earth, to the point of feeling an anxiety thinking about living life without out.

She wasn't sure how long she spent tied up in the boot of car, but she could feel the car twisting and turning. She surmised that the car was speeding up then slowing down at different lights and turnings. She soon lost track of the turnings and genuinely didn't know where she would end up. From what she could hear, they must have driven onto a motorway for a stretch. It was hard for her to guess when she felt so focussed on the act of being his chattel. She settled back in her bondage, wondering what was going to happen to her. She felt a glow of content. An involuntary smile formed on her lips. The contentment came from a feeling of being owned and wanted, by someone she in turn wanted to be owned by. The insatiable desire and slow burning effects of lust he had caused for her, were unfortunately, an occupational bi-product of their relationship, because the aura around him made her feel a maddening, engrossing obsessive love for him. It was a very tentative emotional position to be in, but she couldn't stop herself from stepping off that psychological precipice. It made her feel alive. When it was reciprocated so enthusiastically, it made life feel like paradise. Often, when she felt so overwhelmed by his will, it seemed like the only solution to pursue when she felt this level of intensity in her hunger for him, was to use every part of her being to try and climb inside of him. She entertained this fantasy frequently. It had a way of creeping into her thoughts as a plausible idea. Sometimes deep kissing or impaling herself on his cock would take away some of her longing for him, temporarily. But, she always felt like she wanted more and there was no way to get it. The only other way she could bring herself closer to into him was to carry out his fantasies. Sometimes that helped. It was also what made Stephen so unique to her. She knew he took a great sadistic pleasure in drawing out her longing for him.

Before she met him, life was always the other way around. The men she had known before were always in a hurry to find the quickest route to getting inside her knickers. They had always opted for the "Wham, bam, thank you ma'am" approach to sex in the past. She found that those lacking the skills and carefully considered sexual techniques had served to swiftly bore her. Many former trysts had never amounted to much beyond gathering up her clothes and disappearing in the morning, never to take their calls again. It used to fill her with a mixture of half satisfaction mixed with a little cloud of disappointment. But Stephen was very different. His straightforward and honest approach about his desires was like a gust of pure, fresh air. He wasn't sexually selfish, he was just very direct. What she loved most about him controlling her was the way he knew exactly what he wanted and the way it always had an underlying tone of maximising the amount of pleasure he knew she could receive under his direction. He had a quiet natural power about him that made her instantly feel like bowing to his will whenever she came within a few feet of his presence. He was like a drug that was good for her. She felt so addicted to him, because he understood her. His mind worked in a complimentary way to hers.

The car bumped up and down along (what Lucy guessed must have been) a dirt road. The car eventually came to a stop. Lucy could hear Stephen getting out of the car and slamming the door. Now whistling, his footsteps got closer to the boot. A rush of frosty night air filled Lucy's nostrils. Stephen opened the car boot door widely, studying his helpless chattel inside. She looked up at him, her eyes were filled with love.

'Your face is so fucking beautiful like that,' he said.

He grabbed her by her shoulders to assist her to assume a kneeling position inside the boot. She could see an unfamiliar, tree-lined forest sprawling out before her. The vista of the forest was cloaked in darkness, but the lack of light that she had experienced from being tied up in the boot of Stephen's car made it easy for her eyes adjust quickly. She studied the canopy of trees and saw a panorama of bluey-grey dark hills rising in the distance of the lonely car park. She concluded that she had no idea where they were. Stephen stared straight into Lucy's eyes with a devilish grin.

'Yes, my dear,' he said softly. '... if you are thinking we are out in the middle of nowhere, you are quite correct. So, there's no point in screaming for help. The best thing you can do in this situation is, to be my good girl and do as I say.'

He ran both of his thumbs over her nipples in the cool air until each one stood up on end. Pinching them, he lifted her out of the trunk and led her to sit upright on the edge of the back seat of the car.

A few minutes passed. Soon, tiny pairs of blazing red lights began to appear from the woods. The wind rushed through the trees. Stephen motioned towards the woods with his arm, commanding whatever was lurking in the forest to come forward. Mostly in singles, but sometimes also in pairs, a pack of a dozen large bristling black and grey wolves appeared in the clearing of the car park. Quietly, they padded forward and formed a circle around the couple.

Theatrically, Stephen grabbed Lucy's bra straps and raked them down around her shoulders once again, revealing her firm white breasts to the pack. The first wolf stepped forward and licked her face. With his hot breath and fearsome teeth beside her neck, he drew a broad lick across her nipple. Within seconds he had transformed into half man / half wolf. The others followed suit. They loomed fearsomely around the couple. Lucy watched as their huge, curled canine cocks sprang to attention. Their howls were deafening. Stephen grabbed Lucy's thighs and parted them for the pack. He lifted the fabric of her knickers and nudged it to one side, exposing her pink shaven cunt for all to see. Stephen stepped casually round to the passenger door and sat on the back seat of the car and grabbed Lucy's arms, pulling them tightly behind her. He tore the tape away from her mouth as she stared at the pack of werewolves in fascination.

'Show them, Lucy... Show them how fucking beautiful your face is when you cum,' he said to her.

Lucy laid back in the car, forcing her cunt into the air and acknowledged her own voyeuristic pleasure as she witnessed the first wolf pull himself up to wards her, mounting her.

The force of his animal fucking made her squirm with delirium. Another werewolf snarled and lunged forward, forcing the first one out of the way. He impaled himself deep inside of her pussy with his first stroke. The girth of his cock probed far inside of her and she arched her back, savouring the friction of his thrusts as she felt herself starting towards her first orgasm. She turned her head back and kissed Stephen deeply with insatiable hunger. Lucy watched and wriggled as each werewolf's plunging prick ravished her naked body, howling and grunting as they came. She felt like a communal fuck toy. She was now certain that this was what Stephen had been planning for her all day. No longer being able to contain herself, she squirted heavily across the length of a fifth wolves cock, screaming in orgasm.

'You're my obedient good girl, aren't you?' comforted Stephen. He lifted her out of the back seat of the car and draped her body over the hood. Unleashing his own hard cock, he thrust it pointedly into the highest reach of her arse. With her face pushed hard against the metal, she let out a stifled scream, with the first thrust of his cock plundering the inside of her ass. The werewolves gathered around them. Their tall human-like frames stood ominously above the couple. She felt a massive wolf-like cocks being forced into her mouth from above.

Lucy gasped at the sensation of Stephen's hardness burying itself inside of her. She could feel his orgasm building with every increasing blow from his cock.

'Please sir, please... she pleaded. 'Shoot your load inside of me ... I need it Master.'

Stephen's hard thrusting became even more intense. Another wave of squirting dribbled out of her cunt as the last blow from his prick sent a funnel of hot spunk squelching into the eye of her ass. He rubbed the head of his cock over her pink gaping hole, sighing. As the cum dripped out of her ass, a few of the werewolves lapped up the spunk and pussy juice.

Then, as quickly as the wolves had appeared, they were also gone. The couple found themselves standing alone in the deserted car park. Stephen let Lucy free from her bondage. Exhausted, she put her arms around Stephen and kissed him.

'No one feeds my hunger like you do, Sir' she said with a strong glint in her blazing green eyes.

Stephen smiled to himself with a deep sense of satisfaction.

'And are you still hungry, my dear darkling girl?'

'Always,' she said. 'Always hungry for you... Sir.'

LUNCH

Marla awoke in her plush hotel room to the sound of a loudly buzzing text message. It read:

"Do you still wish to meet me for lunch today? I will be in room 173."

Still half asleep, Marla threw the phone on to the bed. She coupled a yawn with a stretch and smoothed her hand over the long beautiful, brunette tresses of her hair. She peered over the side of the bed to check the status of the slave asleep on the carpet below. A man, clad only in a black leather cock-restraint harness (known as a "gates of hell") lay curled up in a bundle of blankets on the floor beside the bed. Marla had expected him to still be asleep, but he was wide awake. He stared up at her, sporting a thumping erection encased in what resembled a ladder made of leather straps.

'Morning!' Marla said.

'Shall I mask my ugly face for you Mistress?' he whimpered.

'Oh yes of course you should, but I want my heels put on first... then you can conceal your ugly face after. I also want my coffee, slut face, and in that order. Be quick about it! Promptly, slag!' she laughed. Honestly, how can masking the hideousness of your face be more important than bringing me my coffee? Sometimes you can be so me, me, me, honestly."

Her tone with him was almost always offhand and detrimental. The foot-slave looked at her in a way that seemed to treasure every insult she made, when she was considerate enough to make the effort to direct one at him. Marla's long black silk nightgown allowed her to slide to the edge of the bed with ease. This was further lubricated by the midnight purple satin sheets that her footman always made sure to pack for her when she travelled. She swung her feet over the side of the bed and began to wipe them on the hapless slave's face. She smiled as she looked down to observe the soles of her feet. They were still hot and slightly sticky from being buried under the bed covers from her night's sleep. She smiled wickedly as she traced her toes along random interesting locations of her slave's body. Marla giggled with delight, as she poked and pinched at his legs and cock grabbing the skin between her big and first toe.

'Masks, hmm... yes. Masks are an excellent idea,' she mused in a sardonic tone. She lifted her foot from his face and down over his flushed cock before attempting to playfully wedge her big toe into his arsehole. 'You are indeed, truly hideous this morning! I can't quite decide if we should superglue a mask to your face or just go the whole hog and get you plastic surgery, but you really are not fun to look at. I can barely imagine how I shall be able to swallow any food at all today with these gruesome images of your diminished sausage rolling around in my head. Those pictures will be fixed in my mind over the breakfast table. However, the sight of it does amuse me. How funny it is that the most precious part of your body hangs there so vulnerably within such easy reach and access for my pleasure or abuse? What were you thinking when you evolved that way? I struggle with this. If you were the winning sperm out of a race of a billion sperm once upon a time, it's frankly a nightmare to think of what some of the others might have emerged as. I think we would have had to have walled up some of your brothers.

And your cock, it so often reminds me of a cartoon character, but I can't recall quite which one...'

'Madame?' he queried.

'Yes, well... it's pink, it's comical and it constantly exudes a great deal of idiotic, useless nonsense. If someone told me your cock had been created in a Korean animation studio I would find that extremely plausible.'

Marla stared up at the ceiling.

'And yet, on some strange levels. I also like your prick. I have an inner need to torture something and my subconscious always confirms to me that the right thing to torture is your cock. Hmm, strange thought, that.'

She perched on the edge of her bed. Marla pointed down to her slender legs. She poised them for their heels, with toes pointed outward. The sun streamed in through the windows. It made her eyes sparkle with a dark glint that could only be matched by a piece of polished French jet.

The tall, slim, ghost-white skinned creature that Marla liked to refer to as her 'current' slave (*and attendant for everything she needed on a daily basis*) darted across the room. He returned with a pair of seven-inch, black-and-white patent leather heels embellished with wide, post-box red leather ankle straps. The slave gently eased the high heels onto her feet, whilst savouring the aroma of the new leather. She softly rested each shoe on the floor with a little "clack". She enjoyed having her slave assist her in putting them on. She looked down at her gorgeous high heels with a degree of satisfaction. In hushed, reverent tones the slave asked:

'Shall I get my mask now, Mistress?'

'God yes,' she replied, 'I have made as much eye contact with you as I can bear for the day, but you must return immediately with my fresh coffee as soon as you have attended to that.'

Marla looked down to admire her own beautiful legs which were now freshly shod. The shiny, cruel, skyscraper heels gleamed in the morning sunlight. She lay back on the bed, lifting her black satin nightgown up around her hips. It exposed a neatly shaven pussy. She ran her fingers down between her pussy lips to feel her own wetness and the tickling inside of her. She slid three of her fingers down into her cunt and began to work her clit in circular movements as she stared out the window beside her bed. Reaching out with one hand, she drew the curtains open in hopes that someone, anyone in the opposite building might be there to be able to catch the sight of her playing with herself. It was something she loved to do occasionally. When she was spotted by someone it was always a distinctly interesting experience. From her past forays into exhibitionism, she found everyone who had ever witnessed her exploits on her travels were often too embarrassed or confused to say anything about it. She had learned that mostly they would just stare, transfixed in a mixture of voyeurism and shock. It was a situation she took great delight in exploiting. She had hoped that perhaps someone passing a window in the hotel opposite might catch her eye and be able to join in with at least a little bit of her voyeuristic fun. She forced the fourth of her now glistening fingers deep inside her pussy, pushing harder at two-second intervals whilst staring out at the window, still searching for another face in the opposite building. Still, it was to no avail. The windows opposite, were dark and empty.

'Damn it,' she thought. 'I need something interesting to happen to get me excited.'

Marla, now fully unhappy with this lack of audience knelt lewdly on the bed in front of the open window in her seven-inch heels. Her tits spilled out over the top of her nightgown. She he was determined to keep her other hand firmly planted in her pussy hole, as the building pleasure was by now, far too good to let go of. With her other hand, she threw open the sash of the window. She then further hiked her large, ripe breasts all the way out of her black nightdress to perch them on the window sill. Then, kneeling on the bed with her ass raised high in the air, she continued to thrust her fingers in and out of her cunt. Her semi-loud moans managed to attract a willing audience member on the next-over balcony of her hotel.

An older man in a striped bathrobe stood holding a cup of coffee. His eyes were open wide with shock. He stood, open-mouthed and speechless as he watched Marla leaning over the window ledge. As he looked on. One of Marla's hands remained out of sight. That was the hand that was all too busy fisting her own cunt. She spied the area of his crotch where an erection should be but found there to be little going on down there. Marla, now wrapped in her own pleasure, was too distracted to feel a great deal of concern about the circumstances of whether his cock was hard or not. Marla's visible hand pulled at and caressed her windowsill-perched tits with some concentration. After a moment, once she was into a steady rhythm;

she looked up and displayed her tits showily to the man whilst staring directly into his eyes. She smiled triumphantly.

'He would do for now as a brief, morning distraction,' she thought. She threw her head back, continuing to caress her tits and moaned in a low tone, now confident of the torturous effect it would have on the stranger. Her eyes darted between taunting his and closing her lids as they reverted to the sumptuous feeling of her own pleasure. The man watched, transfixed and silent, as though hypnotized

Snapping out of his trance, the man on the balcony pulled his cock out of his white boxers and began to try wanking it. It was obvious that he was trying desperately to get it hard to take advantage of his serendipitous luck.

For a moment, Marla stared over at him, but glanced down at his dick. She formed a cruel yet devious smile.

'Not too much to work with there, your cock?' she tittered in her broad London accent. 'If I were you I wouldn't bother. I would just watch the show...' She let out a dirty laugh that echoed between the exterior hotel walls.

The man in the striped bathrobe fumbled furiously to work the length of his shaft as he stared, transfixed at semi-naked Marla. She could see the moment of disappointment in his eyes that came, when she had insulted him. It made his cock go momentarily soft. She pulled and kneaded her tits for him in what was a mesmerising sight of round, supple flesh and hard nipples. She saw his meagre proportions once again, get stiff. As his eyes met hers she shot him a huge grin. She lifted her breast to her mouth. Smiling, she began to draw her tongue slowly across her own nipple. The man in the stripe bathrobe seemed frozen on the spot. She saw his mouth grow slack with hunger. His breathing became slow and studied. The look on his face showed that he was clearly lusting after what must have looked to him, like the most delicious and unattainable, out-of-reach thing in the world.

Feeling close to the edge of climax, she pulled harder at her breasts and shoved more of her body out of the window. She winced as the cold winds around the building breezed past her, chilling her flesh, but enflaming her cunt. The man craned his neck just enough to catch a glimpse through the window of the sight of Marla working her pussy with her fist. Her moans increased. Suddenly, there was concentrated moment of silence. Marla shuddered as forceful endorphins shot up through her body into her brain. No longer able to hold her orgasm back, Marla screamed. She gasped as she felt an overwhelming sensation of shooting, hard pleasure.

Marla spied down to street level to the hotel doorman who stood below her first-floor room. She had forgotten he might be there. He had been watching all the time. His half smile and cheeky nod gave away totally his knowledge of the scene going on above. His neck was discreetly craned and his eyes held a side glance looking up, but the rest of his stance gave away nothing as people bustled in an out of the main hotel entrance.

'I guess he misses nothing down there,' she whispered, shooting him a little smile.

As Marla relaxed from her orgasm, with plans to collapse back down on the bed. She then caught sight of her slave standing, staring at her, frozen. His face of shock was almost identical to that of the man in the striped bathrobe. His expression was impressive as he was fully masked. His wide-eyed shock was still highly visible under the black leather. In one hand, a steaming hot cup of coffee rattled between his fingers. A small pool of pre-cum had amassed on the floor below him, in line with the position of his cock.

Marla removed her fist from her pussy. She pulled her tits up, away from the windowsill and reached out into the air behind herself. Her hand waved expectantly, extending as it reached for something.

'Coffee now, slave,' she demanded. She continued to look out the window. The slave advanced. Marla grabbed the coffee cup from his hand and took a first sip.

'I didn't give you permission to watch me,' she retorted, collapsing on the bed. 'Now shut the window.'

The slave hopped over to the area beside the bed and rushed to shut the sash. Outside he could see a middle-aged man in a striped bathrobe steadily wanking on the next balcony, craning his neck to consider Marla's window. The two men's eyes locked. Marla glanced out of the window and let out a half smile. She frowned and her eyes rolled.

'Draw the blinds,' she said, as she surveyed the older man. 'Hmm, Oh yes... him. Never mind him. He will shoot his load eventually, I expect. Just let him fizzle out on his own. He's had his chance. Besides,' she taunted, 'I might give him a reprieve a bit later. It might be an opportunity for you to partake a little two-man show for me tonight, tart boy. I might enjoy a little extra entertainment later seeing as you don't seem to know how to or when to ask for permission to watch me. I might coordinate a good manners master class tonight for you both. Sluts like you can always use a bit of instruction in the use of correct etiquette in the presence of a Mistress.'

The slave frowned, making a face of pure dread.

'Perhaps an unexpected guest appearance from that small-cocked bathrobe man might be the way forward to teaching your ogling whore ass what it can and can't do in my presence without my say-so.' Marla clapped her hands together with resolve. 'Might be a plan...' she thought out loud to herself. 'However, I must now be dressed if I am going to meet my newest applicant for my lunch appointment. Chop, Chop! Dress me now,' demanded Marla.

'Yes, Miss Marla,' her naked attendant replied. He scurried about gathering her clothes. She stood behind him pointing and directing as he chose different drawers and garments in her wardrobe.

Marla emerged from the lift of the sumptuous Parisian Hotel. The sign above her head read "Hotel Rêve Noir" as she stepped onto the street. Instantly, with a smile of informed admiration, the concierge quickly hailed a taxi for her. Her tight black satin suit and arm-length black leather gloves were elegantly framed by a full-length black vintage fox fur stole. The fur played seductively around her shoulders and the close-fitting, red silk velvet cloche on her head concealed the mass of neatly trained curls that rested softly around her neck. Her red silk stockings peeped out from under the viciously tight cut of her full-length skirt. Her waist was cinched tightly to an unnaturally tiny size by way of a carefully concealed, steel-boned corset.

From the window her hotel room above, Marla spied her foot-slave looking down to the street. He stared longingly like a lost pup as he watched his Mistress make her impending departure. She threw out a gloved hand and waved up at him. Alone in the hotel room, he stared down at the heavy ball and chain she had attached to his leg. She looked up at him, making a play-acting fist with a smile.

'He's lucky that I only attached that to his leg, and not to his balls today.' she whispered to herself, giggling.

Marla walked to the waiting vehicle. Her heels made a series of sharp, piercing, clacking noises as she walked along the pavement. The sound from her high heels made that would make a few passers-by, stop to do a complete retake. Marla glided towards the waiting car. It was now drawn up beside the curb.

'Take me to Rue De Tempêtes, sixty-nine... er, soixante-neuf, s'il vous plait, Monsieur.' The car pulled away from the hotel into the traffic. As Marla looked out of the car window she could heard the curious sound of the taxi driver huffing mysteriously. He then let out a little muffled groan. Quizzically, she perched herself up on the edge of her seat to see what he could be doing. She observed his his furtive, guilty glances towards the backseat. She fathomed that his glances were accompanied by a familiar movement. It was an action from the taxi driver that told of concealed self-abuse.

'Oh, all these horny men! Not again,' she thought. 'No grace or social skills whatsoever,' she sighed. 'Stop the car! Arrêtez l'automobile! she demanded, in broken French.

The driver, looking vaguely sheepish and a little nervous, pulled over the car and stared at his passenger in the back seat. He was continuing covertly, to pursue his wanking. His eyes kept darting to the space on the taxi floor that was occupied by Marla's silky legs.

'Excusez-moi, Mademoiselle,' he said in a flustered tone. 'Your shoes, they are so beautiful.'

Before he could add anything else to his attempted English dialogue, Marla darted out of the car and slammed the door. Much to his surprise she flung open the driver's door and sat down beside him. She stared at him briefly with a serious look. Softly smiling, she gently retrieved the blatantly bulging cock from his trousers with her leather-clad hand. He smiled at her gratefully, expecting some form of assistance from her.

However, this premise wasn't *exactly* the kind of assistance he had been expecting.

'Not like that!' she directed, rubbing her hands together. 'You do it! Come on, faster... faster! Look, grab the base here!' She motioned a variety of cock-based pantomimes at him with her hands, willing him to attempt to please her despite the obvious language barrier. She enjoyed watching him as he raked his cock, knowing he was flustered by the fact that he was having trouble understanding her. In this instance, Marla didn't care. She knew this action needed little or no fluency in any language to complete. To her, wanking was a universal language. Soon, he was stroking both hands up and down his prick, sufficiently displaying the type of dirty, bizarre show that she seemed to crave of him. Momentarily, her leather-gloved hands ran across his chest. Her fingers ran under the buttons of his shirt, popping each one as she went. Her hands darted and probed around inside of his shirt, pinching and rubbing at his skin.

'Salope!' she whispered. 'Come for me, little slut.' Her hand ran over his cock as she charitably helped him play with it. Soon a froth of white, creamy cum shot out over the top of her gloves. The driver let out a massive groan. She wiped the cum across his face and quickly returned to the back seat of the car. Marla looked down at her gloves and sighed.

'That's another pair ruined,' she thought. 'Rue de Tempêtes soixante-neuf, s'il vous plait Monsieur.' she repeated. Her face showed no emotion. She lit a gold-banded, black cigarette and stared at him disaffectedly. Shrugging and a little dazed, the taxi driver drove on.

Soon the car drew up to the door of a large town house along a brick-lined street. The pathway to the imposing front door was lined with a series of tormented-looking, winged gargoyles. Marla, now sporting a freshly adorned pair of red leather gloves, that she had retrieved from her clutch, stepped from the car and smirked at the taxi driver. She brushed past the contorted and grotesque faces of the statues, and plucked at the antique doorbell. Marla waited for someone to answer the door.

A classically-tailored looking English butler in black mourning coat and grey pinstripe trousers promptly answered the door. With eyes cast down, he offered a hand out for Marla to take as she entered the house.

'May I take your coat, Mademoiselle?' enquired the butler.

'Yes, you may,' replied Marla. 'But I will also take yours if you don't watch out. In fact, yes, remove your coat!' The butler complied with her wishes. His coat concealed a black satin maid's uniform cleverly under his mourning coat. 'Ha-ha,' she giggled. 'You look ridiculous, but I like it.'

Having no coat to remove, she threw her fur stole at the butler's face and took off her suit jacket to reveal a shiny leather bra. The jacket was also sharply thrown into the butler's face.

'Hang that,' she snubbed.

'Thank you, Madame,' he replied with some embarrassment and a little unfamiliarity.

'Marla, Maîtresse Marla ... and you're welcome, *lowlife scum.*' she teased. Her diabolical smile returned. The butler smiled back widely, adoring the painful insult she had levied at him.

Marla walked past the Butler with complete disdain. She had no intention of waiting for him to lead the way for her. She preferred to explore the premises and find the room she required by her own volition. He hopped around behind her, attempting in vain to provide some form of service. Marla just ignored him, acting as ever, like an eternal law unto herself.

The black-and-white tiled halls contained many curious, sexual-sounding muffled yelps. Marla crept from door-to-door, listening intently with ears primped. Groans of pain and pleasure emitted from behind each portal. She sighed at the thought of the delicious images of reamed asses and beaten cocks that were certainly the result of the actions being carried out behind each door. It was wonderful to be back at Rue de Tempêtes. It had well-earned the nickname of "Parisian Mega-Dungeon". For decades, it had been famous amongst the BDSM fraternity as being the place to pursue the most eccentric and extreme fantasies. Soon, Marla stopped at a door that revealed the sound she had been expressly listening out for. She flung the door open.

'Solange!' Marla said as she hurried towards a beautiful, lithe, bleached-blonde, dark-skinned Dominatrix. The woman was clad head-to-toe in a white latex outfit. Mistress Solange had been at the time, busy adding a variety of attachments to the balls of a gagged slave who was strapped down to a dentist's chair in the room. The restrained slave let out a muffled cry. It was quickly stifled by the white latex hand of Solange. She unceremoniously stuffed it into his mouth, mimicking the thrusts of a cock.

'Patience whore, you need to learn patience,' said Solange to the slave.

'Marla!' said Solange. 'I didn't know you were in town! What a wonderful thing it is to see you!' she exclaimed.

The two women kissed. The first light kiss led to a deeper one. Marla unzipped the front of Solange's catsuit and playfully sucked her nipples. Solange sighed.

'I think you should fuck me right now, Marla,' rasped Solange. Solange extended a white latex hand as she pointed to the dentist's chair. 'In fact, I want you to fuck me on top of that slave.' Solange lay down on top of the slave, unzipping the top of her catsuit and spreading her legs. The slave let out a fierce cry of excited anguish as the weight of Solange's large, round bottom purposefully ground itself into the pinching devices that were attached to his cock and balls.

'Avec pleasure, I mean *plaisir*,' said Marla, correcting herself. She walked to survey the walls of medical equipment and kinky toys that were hanging up in the dungeon. She picked up a large, white strap-on dildo and raised her lashes, seeking out the approval of Solange.

'I can take still a little larger than that one,' laughed Solange.

'Oh, really?' said Marla with raised eyebrows.

Marla then chose an enormous, black rubber dildo. It was fixed in place by way of a leather strap-on harness. She buckled it round her waist. Solange squirmed and writhed, ripping her latex body suit open at the crotch exposing her formidable and pretty pussy to give it a good fingering. Solange sighed, drinking in the sight of Marla's amazing body whilst drifting into a warm feeling of lust. It was propelled by the promise of the thrusting from Marla's big strap on that would soon follow. Grabbing her by her hands, Marla held Solange down with a smile and plunged the massive black dildo deep into Solange's wet pussy.

'Aagh!' screamed Solange. 'It's... so big... in my... tiny pussy!' Hungrily, Solange sought out Marla's tongue for some pointed, forceful kisses.

'I love your wet little cunt, Solange.' said Marla with a hiss that accompanied the hard thrusts of the dildo. Marla looked down to enjoy the sight of the huge dildo jabbing in and out of Solange's soaking wet hole.

'Aagh!' came a muffled yell from the slave as the weight of the two women's bodies bore down on his balls. The two girls laughed mercilessly as he writhed around beneath them.

'I so love my Mistress Solange,' mumbled the slave. 'Thank you for letting me serve you both.' The two girls ignored his babbling.

Marla worked the dildo deep into Solange's cunt. Her pussy was now so wet that it made loud squelching noises every time she plunged the giant black rubber prick into her. The exquisite slapping of the hilt of the black dildo against Solange's fuck hole covered the squealing slave below in a deluge of fragrant pussy juice. Marla thrust the dildo deep into her cunt as Solange begged:

'Fuck me harder, fuck me harder! I have been bored to death with this no-dick sissy all day! Remind me what a real fuck feels like, ma Cherie!'

And indeed, Marla did. An orgasm of explosive proportions soon sang out from Solange. Marla looked down and watched with glee as the dildo pushed in and out of her gaping hole, squeezing the orgasm out of her cunt. Solange wriggled with glee, savouring the pressure of the slaves' erect cock between her arse cheeks. Marla plunged her tongue deep into the back of Solange's throat, as she also climaxed.

'Oh... that was so fucking good, Marla,' said Solange.

'Although, I expect your subject learned nothing today,' said Marla as she wiped her dildo on the slave's leg. 'Look at him. His eyes are glazed over!' The two women laughed. Marla poked the slave in the belly curiously with a long red-leather finger. 'Hello? Are you dead? No? Oh well,' she sighed. Almost instantly bored with the catatonic slave, Marla turned her attention back to kissing Solange and the delicious task of caressing the flesh of her formidable bottom.

Solange, now stripping off, pulled on a corded bell beside the door. The butler arrived. He was now dressed as a pink fairy. The two women laughed again.

'We'll take tea in the red room,' said Solange. Now naked, she walked with Marla down the hall, leading her lover the hand.

Shortly after, the butler arrived in the red room with a tray for the two ladies. He knelt on the floor preparing their tea for them. Marla addressed the butler:

'I have an appointment here, actually. Client number 36 in room number one seven three is mine. Has he arrived yet?'

'Yes, Maîtresse Marla. But he is not alone,' replied the butler.

'Oh really? How intriguing,' Solange laughed.

'Well, they can wait...' retorted Marla. 'I will enjoy my tea with you first Solange, my darling.'

When the tea was finished, Marla kissed Solange on the neck and departed. Marla grabbed the butler by the bottom of his frilly skirt.

'Show me the way to room one seven three now,' she demanded. In compliance, he led her along several corridors until they reached a plain wooden door marked "173". The butler gently rapped on the door.

A tall, muscular man in a black leather outfit answered. He was accompanied by another man in a beautifully cut black, designer Italian suit. His eyes were concealed by a pair of sharp looking, dark sunglasses.

A table laid out with plates and sandwiches stood in the centre of a dusty but opulent room. Sun streamed through the rips in the heavy burgundy velvet curtains that hung against the windows.

'Marla?' he asked.

'Yes, Sir...' she replied. 'I believe it's time for lunch,' she smiled.

'Oh yes,' said the man. 'Yes, I believe it is...'

With that, Marla knelt on the floor below the man, facing his cock. She held her face up to his crotch, inhaling the leather and kissing the bulge that contorted beneath the zip. Unzipping his flies, he produced a massive bulbous erection and pushed it hard on her face. She sighed with satisfaction. Roughly he shoved it into her mouth. The other man walked towards them, now aroused by watching. He began stroking his also enormous cock, rubbing it on her face and over her hair. What can only be described as a cock battle took place against her lips as each man took turns dipping their reddened, engorged cocks in and out of her mouth repeatedly. Marla smiled as she felt the force of their huge cocks produce shapes against the inside of her stretched cheek.

'My favourite dish...' she said.

The black suited man began to tease her large, rounded breasts out of her leather bra.

'Very nice...' said the suited man. He began to knead and pull at her breasts with concentrated interest.

'Yes, Master...' she replied.

The leather man said nothing, but continued to rub his cock over her hair and between her tits as she held them together for him. She looked up at him feigning a doe-eyed look for approval. Soon the leather man grabbed Marla's head in his hands and began to thrust his cock in and out of her mouth at a rate that made her feel like she could barely breathe.

Marla winced with pleasure at the intensity of the flavour of the juices from his cock. He pushed her head back with both of his hands. Instantly, she tasted his hot cum shooting into back of her throat. The second man groaned from beneath his sunglasses as he shot his load across her face and hair.

Standing up, Marla smiled at the two spent, post-orgasmic men and began to adjust her clothing.

'That was delicious, gentleman. Thank you for my lunch.' said Marla. Both men grinned, stunned and exhausted.

'So,' grinned Marla, 'what are we doing for dinner?' She laughed.

HALLOWEEN PARTY

Maîtresse Sapphire scanned the morning post over the top of her black, cat-eyed glasses as she sat at her breakfast table. The dazzling rays in her conservatory blazed bright sunshine over the gold threads in the tablecloth. Its shine picked out the gleaming perfection of an ornate antique silver tea service that was laid out on the table. Subtle rainbows swayed across the room as the hanging prisms in the window refracted the light. She unbelted her purple and black silk velvet robe and ran her hand along her neck, rubbing at a muscle.

Sapphire noticed that it seemed inordinately warm for October. When it was too warm, it always meant she had another hot and demanding day of intense beatings in her dungeon to look forward to. She longed for the winter again. The chilly weather did a great deal to help keep her leather dungeon clothing cool. It was especially helpful during those days of hard, corporal punishment she would mete out upon her enthusiastic slaves. Exposure to the frigid air so often also made light work for her corrections of the chattels, as it had the added benefit of making her slave's skin hypersensitive. Her list of high-powered corporate clients would often negotiate for more demanding states of torture from her and she liked to be comfortable whilst she was seeing to her daily activities. Their daily pressures often increased on the approach to the holiday season and it could mean that a very physically demanding period would begin for her. The icy weather was always a good ally for BDSM. In times of wintry weather, she found that locking them in an outbuilding was suitably enough of an ordeal for them that it allowed her to carry on with her other daily concerns without their cries for tighter bondage or a second caning. Locking her chattels in a chilly room with just a bed of straw for comfort would tend to quell the slaves constant bargaining for torment. She enjoyed subduing her slaves whilst simultaneously improving their appreciation of her attention to them.

She pulled a corded bell beside the table. It rang once. A neatly dressed female servant arrived, dressed in a black and white latex maid's uniform, black rubber stockings and white leather, calf length, high-heeled boots.

'How May I serve you Ma'am?' said the maid.

'Please pour out my coffee, Maidy,' said Sapphire. 'Then, be a good girl and lay out my leathers for the day.'

'Yes, Ma'am,' she said. 'I will do that right away. Which leathers would you like me to lay out, please Madame?' she replied.

'Well, as it is autumn. I was thinking perhaps the purple leather thigh length boots, then perhaps the black leather long-sleeved zip up mini dress with the high collar.'

'Yes Ma'am. I will have that ready for you shortly,' replied the maid.

'Excellent, oh yes. Will you try to find the short purple-and-black leather striped gloves? Don't forget that. Be waiting in my chamber to help me dress once you have attended to my coffee.'

'Where should I wait Ma'am?' asked the maid.

'In the kennel, as ever. Off you go. Be a good girl,' the Mistress directed the maid away as she carried on reading her mail.

The maid poured out Sapphire's coffee and added a splash of milk. With a curtsey, she left the room.

Sapphire lifted a cowbell and rang it once. A naked man crawled into the room.

'Oh, do stand up, Rutland, you slut. It's too early in the morning for me to shout down to the floor,' she said with smiling exasperation.

'Yes, "Modom",' said Rutland cheekily.

Sapphire dug her fluffy black kitten-heeled slippers into the slaves back.

Rutland was part slave, part butler and part jester to Sapphire. He secured his position with her by being unselfish and obedient, but he kept it in the long-term because he could make her laugh.

'.. And don't call me "Modom"!' Sapphire chuckled. 'That is too elderly sounding a title for me! I'm not quite *that old* yet, Rutland! I'm only thirty, you know. So, you will address me with a less mocking tone or there will be no public candle wax torture after dinner tonight. You will be made to stay below stairs and not be a party to tonight's BDSM play if you misbehave again … So, what is my correct name?'

'It's Madame...' he said, still wearing a cheeky grin.

'No..' she replied. 'and it's not "Modom" either.'

'It's "Mattress",' he said. His even worse faux-pas was clearly an attempt at insta-punishment.

'Oh!' fumed Sapphire. 'I see. It's like that is it?!'

'No! No!' he exclaimed. 'I meant Maîtresse! I meant Maîtresse!'

'Yes, correct. Get used to it,' she said calmly. 'For that bit of wilfulness, you will get the coloured melted candle wax on your cock tonight instead of the white, which is much hotter, as you know. Honestly, calling me "Mattress!", she laughed. With amusement, she added: 'You should be amazed that I don't have you locked up in the cellar for the rest of your days, I am questioning if you are worthy of being trotted out in polite company.'

'Yes, please, Maîtresse!' exclaimed Rutland excitedly. 'Lock me up forever!'

'Now,' she said. 'I crawled you through here, I mean, *called you through here;* for a purpose. Although, there are days when I hardly see the point of you,' she said sardonically.

'Yes, Maîtresse. How may I serve you?' said Rutland, concentrating.

'You need to open and then read the rest of my post to me,' she stated in a matter-of-fact tone.

Sapphire pulled a large combat knife from a drawer in the conservatory breakfast table and handed it, sharp end, to Rutland. He carefully accepted the knife by its sharp point. He then set about opening her post.

Naked and exposed, Rutland composed himself in the centre of the room as he prepared to read out the first letter. The only accoutrements he seemed to be wearing as attire were a simple, black spiked dog collar and a pair of latex shirt cuffs with added cuff links. Sapphire crossed her legs. Sipping her coffee, she listened to him as he announced her mail.

'Item 1: Electoral Roll. Please sign this document and state all of the occupants and dependants living at this address.' announced Rutland.

'Hmm, I think it will be just me voting again this year. Yes, just me. Seeing as you and the maid have no rights or validity that seems acceptable. Fill that in, sign it and post it today. However, if I listed you and the maid as living here and arranged a postal vote. I could vote three times,' she mused. 'Next missive, please,' she ordered.

Rutland opened the next letter. It's from Scotland. It appears to be one of your postal slaves.

'Well, what is he saying?' she enquired.

Rutland put on a comedy Scottish accent.

'He has written, "It's a braw bricht moonlicht nicht the nicht, please kick me in the prick, ocht aye!" A smile curled across Rutland's naughty looking, middle-forties aged face.

Sapphire laughed again.

'Rutland read my mail properly! Honestly, I don't know why I bother sometimes,' she said. 'You won't be giggling later when I have covered your scrotum in slow-drying cement! I wish you weren't so fearless sometimes. You positively slow down the machinations of this household with your nonsense,' Sapphire giggled and lifted a cigarette. Rutland hopped over to her, still grasping the letter in his hand. With his other hand, he lifted a lighter from the table and lit her cigarette. He beamed at her with a charming smile. Then, returning to his original position; he continued to read the letter.

'Item 2: It seems to be saying that he wants his key back,' said Rutland, studying the letter.

'His key to what?' she enquired.

'...The key to his chastity device. It seems he has met a Scottish Dominatrix up in Glasgow and she seems to be requesting the key to his cock,' replied Rutland.

'Hmm.' said Sapphire. 'Well I have no problem selling him on, that's fine with me. Tell him the price of his key five thousand pounds sterling. Oh Rutland, do find out the name of the Mistress and do a background check on her, then pop my price in a letter to him and let him know upon completion of the sale the key will be posted out to his new Mistress for his future supplication,' she said calmly.

'Yes, Mistress, I will attend to that letter this afternoon,' said Rutland.

'Good bunny, you'll get high quality torture later for that as a "thank you",' said Sapphire. 'Now, on to the next letter! Come on, let's hear it!'

Rutland opened the large brown envelope to reveal a copy of a fetish magazine. He held it up and looked at his Mistress.

'Shall I read *all* of this out?' he asked.

'No just go to the back pages. I believe I have advertising at the back. I want to see exactly where they placed it and how it looks,' she replied. 'You can read *that* out when you find the ad, though.'

Rutland flipped through the magazine until he reached the back pages and the advertising section. His eyes fell upon an image of his Mistress. The picture was a very good one. She was wearing a neck-to-toe black latex catsuit and crimson red spiked boots. Rather than being seated with traditional Dominatrix style majesty on her dungeon throne, she had cradled herself sideways into the chair. Her legs were crossed casually and dangling over one side. In one of her gloved latex hands she held a cigarette on a long holder. In the other hand, she held a kneeling slave wearing a jack-o'-lantern mask by his hair to face the camera. In large, scary, horror-themed orange letters the words "Halloween Special" was written underneath her image. The small text was unusual. Rutland continued to read her magazine ad.

'Item 3: This month's Halloween special will get your true fears flowing as ghosts, spooks, vampires, werewolves and fearless slaves are all welcome to sample the delights of the world's most truly demonic Mistress. You are invited to take up the challenge of visiting Britain's sexiest haunted house: the dungeon of gothic sadist Maîtresse Sapphire. Quote the words "Trick or Treat" upon arrival and get free verbal humiliation and an extra unspecified mystery torment with every session.'

'That's a very good advert Mistress,' said Rutland.

'Well, it's my favourite holiday. It's the most fun time of the year for me. It's like gothic Christmas! I like to get a little bit of a holiday theme going, you know,' she said cheerfully. 'The torture chamber always looks better at this time of the year. It's a compliment to the moans of suffering flesh. Now, pour out the rest of my coffee, Rutland. Mail call is over. There's that big bag of Halloween decorations under the stairs. I want you to go put them up in the dungeons. Now, off you pop, hussy.'

Draining the last of her coffee, Sapphire began to climb the double staircase leading to her bedroom to dress for the day. As she walked through the heavy oak door, she glanced across to an ornate wooden cage in the corner of the room. Inside, her latex maid was curled up staring expectantly at Sapphire. The leather outfit she had requested was laid on the bed. She snapped her fingers and patted the top of her thigh.

'Heel, Maidy,' she said, stripping off her black robe. 'It's time to help me dress.'

Sapphire stood towering above the little latex maid, wearing only a sheer black thong and a pair of stockings. To the maid, Sapphire looked much like a kinky paper doll. Her large pale breasts dangled ominously above the shy maid.

'Dress me, knickers first, then stockings. I also want to wear leather suspenders. Top drawer, right side please Maidy,' she demanded.

The maid scurried towards the wardrobe and returned with the garments that she had been directed to fetch for her Mistress. Gently, the maid began to delicately dress her in a new pair of stockings and the short leather dress. Sapphire sat down on the bed to watch as the maid laced her into her purple leather thigh boots. The maid fluttered her eyelashes at her, blushing a little.

'May I say how beautiful you are looking today, Mistress?' said the Maid.

'Maîtresse, you know I prefer that. Please be a good girl and use the correct terminology. But, thank you for the compliment,' retorted Sapphire. Now standing to her heels, Sapphire towered a further six inches in height above the young slave maid.

'You know,' she said. 'My boots are not looking as glossy as I would like them to be, girl. I think you should clean them.'

The maid winced. She stared at the boots and noticed indeed, they were not as highly polished as they should have been. Sapphire looked down at the maid's slightly guilty-looking face and pointed towards her boots. The maid, knowing exactly what was expected of her, began to lick them clean.

'I want you to lick them as hard as you can, girly,' said Sapphire. She lifted her boot and shoved it towards the maid's mouth. Then grabbing the maid's head by her champagne pink hair, she proceeded to force the maids face into the taut black leather of the dress that was stretched across her ass.

'You can lick that too, you little slut,' she said devilishly.

Sapphire turned and grabbed the maid by the neck. She raised her up off the floor. She grasped the ruffled sleeves of her latex maid's uniform and yanked it down to reveal a pair of pert little breasts. She pinched them until they became hard.

'I think you can go about your duties today like this,' she said with an evil smile. 'It will be fun watching you answer the door to our callers and attending to your duties this way.'

The maid felt a surge of shame. The thought of answering the door all day to a plethora of clients and strangers whilst being topless would be difficult to achieve. She was used to only ever being naked in front of her Mistress and occasionally, Rutland. But she was keen to please her Mistress. Being relatively new to her position as "personal maid", she nodded compliantly.

The now-dressed Sapphire headed to her office to look at her schedule for the day. On the wall calendar of the office, Rutland had written up the names and arrival times of all her visiting clients and appointments.

'Hmm. I have my first victim in thirty minutes. It seems that he is early. Oh well, albeit for me to be one to question the best time of the day for torture. As far as I am concerned, all times of the day are acceptable,' she thought.

Lighting a cigarette in her purple leather gloves, she descended into her cellar dungeons and hit the intercom. It was attached to a walkie-talkie that was attached to Rutland. He was busying himself with a feather duster in the large, black and cream tiled entrance hall.

'I am ready to receive my clients now. Do let me know when this first one called 'Griffin' arrives.'

'Yes Ma'am,' replied Rutland.

'Unusual name,' thought Sapphire.

After a few minutes, Sapphire heard as the door chimed loudly above her in the hallway. The client appeared to be dead-on time. She heard the cellar door open and a pair of heavy footsteps descend the stairs. A man entered the room. He was of average height, but very stocky with a strong jawline. Sapphire smiled at him.

'Welcome,' she said pleasantly.

'Trick or Treat,' said Griffin.

'Ah yes, you little cockless looking hairball,' she laughed. 'I remember, the verbal humiliation. I expect in a few minutes you will be stripping off to show me your pitifully useless shrivelled prick and boy pussy for a much-needed shafting. That said, it's hard to say if you would survive a seeing-to, because you look like a complete virgin,' she laughed sadistically.

'Yes, Mistress,' said Griffin. 'What would you like me to do?'

'Stripping is customary,' she said. 'I want to examine your flesh to ensure you are not as completely as repulsive as I suspect you are. Thankfully I am wearing the gloves today, so even if you are repulsive, I can at least take comfort in the knowledge that my flesh will never have the misery of touching yours. It's better if I use long-range implements to deal with you instead.'

The blood drained from Griffin's face as he began to take off his clothes. He hadn't been expecting such extreme verbal humiliation from the offset.

'Put your hands on your head,' said Sapphire.

Slowly, she circled the submissive. His eyes followed her closely as she studied and caressed his body closely. With both hands, she grabbed his arse roughly.

'Nice firm bottom you have there, Griffin,' she said with a cheeky grin. 'I will enjoy beating that black and blue later. Now, I think you should kneel down.'

Sapphire lifted the skirt of her leather dress and forced her black leather v-string towards his face.

'Smell my pussy and then lick the leather, slut,' she said. She shoved his head towards her knickers with a gloved hand.

Griffin inhaled deeply and felt immediately that his cock was getting hard. He began to lick the tiny slip of fabric. Her fragrant perfume of honeysuckle mixed with the smell of new leather overwhelmed him.

Sapphire lifted a spiked, red leather dog collar from the wall and fastened it around his neck, attaching it to a lead.

'Come with me, but stay crawling,' she said sternly.

Griffin followed. She led him to a shiny black bondage bench. She made him lay across it with his arse facing upwards. He gazed into a mirror on the wall in front of him. He observed the Mistress as she tightly fastened several black leather belts attached to the bondage bench across his torso. She then used the lower straps on the legs of the bench to tighten his ankles and wrists. Sapphire lifted the silver chain dog lead that hung down from his collar. She placed it in his mouth.

'Do look after this, dog boy,' she said. She ran her leather hands along his body. Firmly, she whacked his ass with a blunt type of trauma rather than a sting. The bondage bench that he was strapped to, shook with the force.

'I feel like getting right into an intense session from the outset, but you still need a little warming up first,' she said. She watched as a pink glow formed on his bottom in the shape of the slaps that thudded across his backside. Griffin squirmed as darker red hand prints started to appear on his rump. She lifted a silver-tipped riding crop from the rail of equipment. The equipment was carefully organised according to size and length on her dungeon wall. With a sharp swing, the solid piece of leather whizzed through the air and landed across his back. Griffin jumped and screamed.

'Owww!' he yelled, spitting out the dog leash.

'If you yell like that again, I am going to have to seek the ball gag,' she retorted with a smile.

She lashed the crop over his back several more times.

'Your body looks so much better covered in marks like that. It seems to me that your flesh is meant to be kissed in many, diverse ways,' she mused.

She turned the crop around and began to rub the silver tip along the whip marks on his back. He let out an anguished scream. Ignoring his cries, Sapphire ran the tip of the silver crop down the lines of his back before wedging it into his asshole.

'Arrrrrgghh!' cried Griffin. He twisted and turned on the bondage bench. Sapphire forced the crop further up his arse. He let out a tortured howl that Sapphire was taken aback by. Leaving the crop still wedged inside her vulnerable victims' sphincter, she stepped back to look in the mirror to observe his face and survey the situation. To her complete amazement; fangs appeared from the mouth of the tied man and hair began to sprout across his back. A swirling blackness engulfed him. Her eyes widened and she took in a sharp breath. She watched as he sprouted the enormous grey brush of a fluffy tail and pointed ears. His face elongated. His body was now covered with mottled tufts of white and grey fur.

'How strange,' she thought. Her attitude to all things unusual was often that of a lack of shock. 'He appears to be a werewolf. It must have been the silver tip of the crop up his arse that shook that loose.'

Griffin let out a long, low tormented howl. If Sapphire had been upstairs when that had happened, she would have witnessed her maid and her butler Rutland frozen on the spot. Their faces registered an equal amount of shock, as they stood bolted to the floor of the locations from where they had been working.

'Hmm. A submissive werewolf,' she said. 'Now, that's not in the manual,' she laughed. 'I guess I will have to write it in, or perhaps get a kinky veterinarian on standby for this kind of eventuality in future.'

Sapphire noticed that he had broken through his restraints. So, she lifted the biggest spiked dog collar she that she possessed from her rack of equipment and fastened it around the werewolf's neck. Sapphire released the remainder of the intact straps from the bench, as his frame no longer fit the equipment in a practical way. Carefully, she led him over to her black and silver bondage throne so she could get a better look at him. The werewolf followed her quietly. When he tried to resist her pulling at his collar; she would give it a sharp tug. She sat down on the chair and cast a long glance across his canine frame. Not missing a beat, with the toe of her shiny boot she began to rub Griffin's cock. The sinews of the muscle that defined his half human/ half wolf body were highly sculpted and beautiful to look at. She found it unusual that the colour of his eyes had changed from deep brown to a dazzling light blue. She watched carefully as his large, tube-like werewolf cock began to harden. Large drops of alien-looking clear pre-cum began to drip from the end.

'Good dog,' said Sapphire. 'Let's see what you can do with that tongue of yours as well.'

Sapphire parted her legs and pulled the werewolf's chain towards her. Nudging the leather fabric of her black knickers to one side, she ordered him to cowl beside her.

'Lick my pussy,' she ordered. 'Hmm, a dog being made to lick a pussy, this seems rather egregious.'

With huge lapping motions, the werewolf began to hungrily lick the Mistress as was ordered. Sapphire squirmed. The scale and force of Griffin's tongue against her thighs was more intense than any other state of pussy eating that she had ever encountered before. The length of his tongue reached right almost into the top of her pussy hole and she could feel the beginnings of a violent orgasm building within her. Griffin began to whine. The power of his licking was creating a force inside of him that made him feel desperate to mount the Mistress. He felt like his animal instincts were taking over. He could feel his will beginning to break ranks away from his Mistress-and-slave relationship with her. Sapphire parted her legs widely. Within a flash he plunged his werewolf cock deep inside of her pussy. He began humping her violently against her throne. Sapphire relented. The bizarre opportunity she found herself accepting was by far overshadowed by the sheer pleasure of Griffin's skill at filling her pussy with a hard, satisfying fuck.

Sapphire grabbed the back of the throne to gain more purchase as she pushed her thighs hard towards his cock. With a few slow stabs, he looked down at her and watched her face as it contorted insanely with orgasmic pleasure. Her mind filled with disjointed scenes of her own image of being fully fucked on her throne by a werewolf. Her cunt became swollen as she thought lasciviously about the fact that it was now filled with half human, half dog cock. She felted crazed as she thought about what his cum must taste and look like. She felt a moment of burning in her mind, as a highly-charged orgasm took over her senses at the front of her brain.

Sapphire screamed. A shower of female ejaculant flooded out over Griffin's cock. The throne was now saturated in her pussy juice. She could feel Griffin's fur was sodden from her orgasm. She felt a further rip of her stockings as the werewolf began to ravage her pussy. A strange sensation of something that felt much like a balloon began to fill her cunt. She watched the scene above her as she experienced a piping hot funnel of what felt like a gallon of cum shooting up her pussy. He let out a deafening howl.

'OowwOOOOOOOOOoooh!' he howled relentlessly. His cock stiffened one last time as every drop of spunk drained from his balls. He slumped to the floor.

Sapphire composed herself. She walked over to the intercom and buzzed it a couple of times. After a few moments, her maid reappeared. The top of the maid's uniform was still pulled down at half mast, still exposing her pert little breasts.

'Yes Ma'am?' she asked politely.

'Clean me up Maidy,' she ordered.

The maid fell to her knees at the throne and began to lick the cum out of Sapphire's pussy.

'And don't forget to swallow,' said Sapphire blankly staring at the ceiling.

At the side of the throne a black mist revealed the shivering body of the naked slave. He had transformed himself back into the guise of a human male.

Sapphire stood up and walked over to Griffin. He looked up at her, his newly brown eyes still held their wolf-like gaze. His body lay quaking from the amount of physical exertion that he had just experienced. She lifted his now loosened collar and stared into his face coldly. She ran the tip of the silver cane a few inches away from his lips.

'Now I want you to show her what you can do, as well,' she said with a glow of post orgasmic pleasure.

Griffin started to attempt to speak to raise protest. But as soon as the silver of the cane had touched his lips it was too late. Sapphire now knew his secret and she had every intention of exploiting it yet again. She grabbed the maid and threw her to the ground.

'Get on all fours, Maidy. I have a present for you,' she teased.

The maid's eyes widened as she watched the slave transform into a huge, hulking werewolf once again. The Mistress lifted the maid's skirt and peeled away her latex knickers. It made a faint smacking sound. She grabbed the chain on the werewolf's collar and pulled him into position on top of the maid. She watched again with a scientific interest as his massive tube-like canine cock stiffened.

'This is fascinating,' she thought. 'I am going to need a veterinary manual for future reference about this. I had no idea.'

She watched gleefully as the tormented Griffin plunged his enormous cock into the tiny maid's wet slit. This time, she was the one to let out a low and agonised howl. Sapphire stood back and watched with delight as the werewolf pumped her maid with his hardened cock. She also quietly congratulated herself on her keen consideration for broadening the maid's sexual experiences, whilst admitting that it was also an incredibly pleasurable spectacle to watch. The sight of the leathery fur and muscular sinews of flesh humping her helpless maid made her feel hot all over again. Her maid whimpered. Sapphire turned to look the maid straight in the eye. She placed an affectionate kiss on her lips. The maid's eyes rolled into the back of her head in ecstasy.

'Fuck her harder!' demanded the Mistress. 'I want you to fuck her twice as hard as you fucked me! Beg for it, maid,' she went on, 'Beg the doggy to pump you full of it's spunk, because you are a dirty little slut and you know it.'

'I'm begging!' screamed the maid. 'I can feel his dog prick filling me up, Mistress.' she gasped. 'Please, I want to feel you cum inside of me. I'm begging you, please.'

Griffin roared again. Her girlish hunger and pleading created a huge surge of arousal. He looked down to view his cock plundering the furthest regions of her tiny cunt. He could feel her pussy contract against the force of his swollen prick, trying to push it out as he thrust it back in repeatedly. He could feel the volcano of pressure building at the base of his balls and let out a furiously long, drawn-out howl. A tower of cum shot up inside of the maid's pussy from his penis. The maid lurched forward to the floor, contorting in orgasm. Griffin quickly took his cock out of her pussy and shot the remaining drops of his load over her ass. She screamed again. He slumped down on top of her, now even more exhausted. After a few moments, the black swirl of fog returned; transforming him back into his human form.

The Mistress stood up. She laughed a little, as she observed the carnage of spunk that had drenched the floor around her throne.

'Look at this place!' she exclaimed. 'This maid certainly has her work cut out for her today. '*When* you can walk again, Maidy,' she started.

'Yes Miss,' replied the maid in a weak, yet still-obedient tone.

'*When* you can stand up,' she said expectantly, 'I want you to go upstairs and clean yourself up, then get the cleaning implements down here to sterilise my workspace for my next visitor.'

'Yes, Miss,' the maid replied. Her voice sounded drained.

'Maîtresse!' she giggled, reminding the maid.

Sapphire walked over to the dazed 'wolf' slave, as he lay depleted on the floor.

'I expect he will come around in a minute or two,' she said to the maid. 'When he wakes up, get him upstairs and give him a fresh bowl of water... and maybe some biscuits. Slowly, the maid hobbled carefully up the staircase to carry out her new task.

The maid returned, with trug basket full of cleaning products and began to sterilise the space. Sapphire wiped a small globule of spunk from the cock of the spent former werewolf, tasting it.

'Unusual flavour,' she said to herself. 'It tastes rather like chicken soup.'

The maid tidied the dungeon area to its' former state of cleanliness. Sapphire watched as the slave stood up and began to dress in his clothing.

'Thank you,' said the slave. 'That was excellent.'

'Yes, that last howl really hit the spot,' she said with a hint of a smile.

Sapphire's ears perked up. She heard the doorbell ringing upstairs.

'Well,' she said politely. 'I guess that's my next appointment. I hope you will come back and see me again soon, so we can explore this further. I find you quite fascinating, but also a cheap dirty whore. Therefore, you are welcome to visit anytime.'

Upstairs, Rutland sauntered across the tiles of Sapphire's large hallway to answer the bell. He pulled the door open and stared at the doorstep in disbelief. Before him stood a pack of five large, male wolves with blazing blue eyes. Their eyes glinted. Silently, they filed past him and headed for the cellar door. The lead wolf looked up at Rutland. With a slight look of confusion, Rutland opened the door and showed them in with his trained formality. They calmly descended the staircase towards the dungeon. The wolves quietly entered the room and stared first at the wolf-slave, and then at Sapphire.

'Trick or Treat' said Griffin with a broad smile. Sapphire smiled back.

'Trick or Treat indeed,' she said. 'Is that what that last howl was for?

'Yes,' he replied. 'We were hoping you would be the right one to indulge all of our fantasies, Mistress. But I had to be certain.'

Sapphire stared up at the ceiling and hit the intercom again.

'Rutland! Tell that maid to get her butt back down here, I'm going to need some help! And bring down the latex sheeting whilst you are at it! And, cancel my other appointments for the rest of the day!' she ordered. 'Rutland! Don't forget to look out the coloured candle wax. You are still scheduled for hot wax torture later this evening!' She turned to spy the lustful-looking wolf pack with a degree of amusement.

'I do love Halloween,' she said, with a raised eyebrow. She watched as the howling mass of wolves transformed into large pack of grizzled werewolves. Sapphire knelt to the floor. She grabbed two of the werewolves' cocks in each of her still-wet gloved, leather hands. She began to suck on them in turns.

'Now I wonder, what *their* cum tastes like,' she thought to herself. 'And I wonder how much stamina my maid has for this as well. I guess I am about to find out. I do hate to break ranks. But this is all just too fascinating to miss,' she thought. She watched the cocks of the looming dog-like figures begin to harden above her.

'It seems every dog has his day, and I guess today is yours,' she said to the creatures.

SHOPPING

Ava found a bench to sit on in the town square. She found herself to be visiting a small village that day. She sipped on a cup of hot takeaway tea and smoked a cigarette, as she watched the locals busy themselves to-ing and fro-ing around the square. She could see that they were attending to their errands and chatting to other passers-by. She patiently waited for her friends to arrive. The town square was wide and expansive with a mixture of new and antiquated buildings. They seemed to be fused together in very incongruous ways. Her walk through this unfamiliar town had been a lot quicker than she had expected it would be. She had briefly perused the goods in a few of the vintage clothing shops and peeped through a few boutique's windows but didn't feel massively compelled to investigate any them further, as nothing interesting had managed to catch her eye. She was used to shopping in London, where there were endless high streets, boutiques and market stalls. Having so much access to a plethora of diverse shops had made her become very selective, when it came to picking out the kind of things that she would want to shop for. She looked a little bit out of place in her fitted black frock coat, black leggings, black leather knee boots and white bug-eye sunglasses. The locals were dressed much more conservatively, but the security of her sunglasses gave her the freedom to look around at this strange place and not care about the people who noticed her unusual dress. She could see that some were staring at her with either a scowl of disapproval or foreign curiosity.

Her phone buzzed with a text message:

'Hey,' was all it read.

Ava had been running a fetish club for several years. She was used to the conditions that allowed random people to have access to her mobile phone number. This was due to the amount of flyering and advertising in kinky magazines that she had undertaken previously. She found the random messages at times oddly entertaining and often responded when she felt the whim take her fancy. She decided to reply.

'Who's that?' she typed back.

'Your little bitch,' came the reply.

Ava stared at the message, racking her brains. This latest conundrum made her try to remember if there were there were any kinky escapades that she may have been engaged in recently where a text like that might make more sense, but she couldn't recall anything significant.

'Which "my little bitch" are you? Please be more specific,' she typed.

'It's J.J. Have I been Naughty? Are you going to spank me, Mummy?' replied J.J.

'Don't call me Mummy. I have no idea who you are and I am not into Mummy scenarios. Texting strangers like that is a bit creepy,' she mashed the message quickly into the phone keypad.

'Please don't blackmail me,' came J.J.'s reply.

'Blackmail you?' she returned. 'Interesting. Send me a dirty picture of you,' she typed.

After a few moments, a picture message came through on her phone. It was a picture of a man's legs and torso dressed in stockings and sheer knickers.

'That was hot,' she typed. 'Send me another one.'

A second picture buzzed though. It was of a gloved woman's hand next to a cock. Someone was covering it with several clothes pegs.

'Mm,' typed Ava. 'I liked that. Now send me one of your face and your cock. Send me a picture of you naked.'

J.J. sent another pic. This time he was on his knees. A large, imposing Mistress clad in a red latex dress stood towering above him as he sucked her black leather strap on. The dildo attached to it was enormous. She could see that he was playing with himself as he sucked.

'Now, that *is really* hot,' she returned in her message. 'I'll bet you really felt humiliated doing that, like the little bitch you are. Did she fuck you with that giant cock after?'

'Yes, Mistress,' replied J.J. 'I felt very low and demoralised after that.'

'Good,' typed Ava. 'I wouldn't mind degrading you in an equivalent way. Except I would do it at an afternoon tea party with all my other Mistress friends watching. You would be our little fetch-and-carry bitch for us. Then we would take turns fucking you and making you service us.'

'Mistress, that would be like a dream come true for me,' replied J.J.

'Well, good. Are you on social media? Why don't you friend me so we can arrange that sometime very soon? I am due to hold another tea party in a few weeks. You'll find me under "Ava Von Ravensberg".

'I will do it now,' replied J.J. 'Oh, Miss... I am so excited at the thought!'

Ava looked at her phone as one of her social media apps popped up with the notification of a friend request from someone called "Jimmy Black". She accepted. In the messaging service within the social media app, she sent "Jimmy Black" a new message:

'Those pics made me really horny. Have you got a few more? I liked the naked ones of you serving that Mistress. Send me some more like that.'

Ava watched her phone as image after image flooded into her message box. There were six in total. She then perused Jimmy Black's profile to see what could be done with it. She looked over his social media page and quickly read that he was married and from Birmingham, that he worked in construction and was an avid supporter of Manchester City football club. She called up his friends list and briefly cross-checked his family and friends. It appeared to be his legitimate social media profile. More interestingly one of the friends on his list was his wife. His wife had been clicking "like" on most of his posts.

She went back to her messaging service and perused the new smutty images she had been sent from J.J. (or 'Jimmy Black'). The first picture showed him wearing a frilly blue hat and matching panties as he sucked his thumb. His hard cock strained against his feminine light-blue knickers. The next one showed him kneeling side on, on all fours with a dildo shoved up his arse as he stared into the camera. One of her favourite pics depicted him spread-eagled across a bed in a random dungeon. He was ball-gagged and tied to the bed. The pointed heel of a shiny red ankle boot was planted firmly on his balls.

'Nice pics J.J.,' Ava typed to him. 'You really are a dirty slut.'

'Yes, Mistress. I am a slut. I want to be *your* slut.'

'Well, I don't know about that J.J.,' replied Ava. 'I mean, here you are sending random dirty texts to a stranger. And you are clearly filthy beyond repair. I am just sitting here wondering what your wife, all your friends at work and all your little football friends would think about you in that frilly hat and panties. I might have to post all these pics to your wall just to teach you a lesson, or maybe just send them directly to your friends. That way you will never know who has which pics about you.'

'No, Mistress! Please don't!' replied J.J.

Ava clicked on the 'add friends' button in her app. She requested J.J.'s wife 'Mary' as a friend.

'I've just added your wife as a friend,' she returned to J.J. 'If you don't want me to share all your dirty pics with her. I suggest you start complying with my wishes.'

'What wishes, Mistress?' asked J.J.

'I haven't decided yet. But I expect it will be money or lingerie or a holiday. I'll get back to you on that later. Oh, that's nice. Your wife just accepted my friend request! Now do be a dear and go get her some nice flowers. I will deal with you later. Got to go now. Bye,' she typed.

'Mistress?' J.J. replied.

Ava ignored his message, let out a chuckle and put the phone back in her pocket.

Ava looked up and smiled as she saw her two friends walking towards her. It was an older man and a lady in her late thirties.

'Was that message anyone good?' asked the lady.

'I have no idea if he's any good or not, but I expect I will find out eventually,' answered Ava. The lady gave her a sideways glance. 'I have so many random text messages and enquiries from one day to the next that I never quite know what is around the corner next.'

Mark and Paris were a hot-looking couple. Paris was petite and blonde. She was of Dutch extraction. Her dark avant-garde style of dress made her look very different to the other locals in the village square. The heavy black make-up around her eyes gave her the look of a Japanese cartoon. Mark, stood five feet nine inches and portrayed a bulky stature. His defined body was nicely framed by a pair of tight camouflage trousers and black military boots. Despite looking and dressing like that of an ex-army paratrooper, there was a sweet smiling glint in his large brown eyes that always had a way of disarming any female or male as he zoomed past them at speed. That was part of what Ava found attractive about Mark and Paris; no matter where she met them, she always delighted in witnessing the trail of heads turning as the two swaggered down any road.

'Lovely to see you Ava,' said Paris as they kissed each other on both cheeks. 'So, what's on the menu for today?' she asked.

'Well,' replied Ava, 'I spied an interesting-looking, sort of Mod Shop full of vintage clothing back there. I wondered if we could just pop in before we go back to yours.'

'Yeah, sure. No problem.' replied Paris, as Mark followed quietly behind them.

The trio entered the shop. Ava gave a cheeky smile to the girl behind the counter. 'Hello!' she said warmly.

The girl behind the counter beamed back. She was another petite girl with long chestnut brown hair and a straight fringe that raked tightly across her forehead. Her pale pink lips made a heavy contrast to her smoky black make-up as she buzzed around the shop pricing items in her bright orange and white mini dress accented by white patent leather knee boots. Her look was very fitting for the retro feel of the shop.

'If there's anything I can help you with, let me know.' said the girl.

The girls nodded back.

'Okay if we look out back?' said Paris.

'Yes, of course,' replied the shop girl. 'There's a changing room too, in case you might want to try anything on.'

'Thanks.' replied Ava.

The two girls began to peruse the racks of clothing at the back of the shop. They were crammed with old leather coats, wild coloured dresses in acid prints. An outlandish-looking pink chiffon cocktail dress was draped over a tailor's dummy.

Paris lifted a garment out of the rack.

'Ava!' she exclaimed. 'Look at this!'

Paris held up an electric blue and white nylon negligee from the nineteen seventies era. It had a sheer matching robe attached to the hanger. The two girls laughed.

'Now that's an outfit you would wear to seduce the milkman,' said Ava.

Paris laughed. 'Without a doubt,' she replied. 'I think one of us should try it on.'

'I will!' said Ava enthusiastically. 'Then we can see what Mark thinks.'

The two girls walked into the back room with the garment and into the changing cubicle. Ava stripped down to reveal her little round breasts and pink g- string. She had toenails and nipples to match. Paris slipped the negligee over Ava's head.

'Mark!' called Paris. 'Get back here and tell us what you think of this dress.'

Mark looked over to the counter girl and rolled his eyes as he skulked to the back of the shop.

Ava stood in full view of the mirror in the cubicle. Her beautiful lithe frame was outlined by a mist of electric blue vintage chiffon as Paris knelt beside her, clinging to her thighs.

'Come here Mark.' said Ava.

'I want you watch something.' Mark stood transfixed and Paris began to thrust her fingers under the tiny scrap of fabric that was Ava's g- string. Paris began to use her fingers to gorge her Ava's pussy. Mark drew in a breath. Ava turned around with a smile to reveal the pink satin strap of her thong rising between her arse cheeks. Paris nudged the strap to one side.

'I want you to lick Ava, Mark,' demanded Paris.

Mark felt his cock flush to a full erection instantly. Panicked and worried about discovery from the shop girl, he glanced over his shoulder to the doorway that led back to the main part of the shop. Both girls craned their necks towards him displaying the beauty of their skin. They looked him straight in the eye with expectation.

'Now, 'demanded Ava.

Mark rushed into the cubicle and dropped to his knees. He buried his face into Ava's arse.

'Come on now, Mark,' whispered Paris. 'I've seen you try harder than that. Force your tongue in.'

Mark pushed his tongue into Ava's ass to its full extent. He searched for the darkest reaches of Ava's pink rosebud as she bent over forcing her cheeks roughly into his face. Ava had every intention extracting the maximum of purchase from his tongue.

Paris, still fingering her cunt reached over and rubbed her hand across the fabric that strained against Mark's cock.

'Mm,' said Ava. 'Good boy, keep it up,' she said smiling. Ava could feel her body tingling, laced with pleasure.

Ten minutes passed in the cubicle. It seemed like torment for Mark; he was terrified of discovery. At the same time, he felt the frustration of knowing that this event could not be taken any further than it currently was, in these surroundings. All this activity left him aching to fuck the two women, who in turn were doing everything they could think of to drive him insane.

The sharp crack of metal scraped along the changing room rail as the shop girl flung the curtain open. Ava smiled. Paris pouted with the look of a guilty pup. Mark's face turned red with complete embarrassment.

'What's going on here?' shouted the shop girl.

Mark, flustered. 'We, we were just trying this dress on, and ...'

'And what?' shouted the shop girl. 'You decided to turn my shop into a whore palace?'

'No, Miss,' stammered Mark. 'We just ...'

'There's no excuse for this!' boomed the shop girl. 'I am calling the police. I am going to tell them you are a filthy sex pervert and you've tried to bring prostitutes into my shop for your own perverted games. Then I am phoning the local paper. Everyone in this town is going to know what kind of disgusting pervert you are.'

'No! Please Miss. Please don't do that!' pleaded Mark. I'll do anything to make it up to you. It was an accident. I didn't mean to disrespect you or your shop!'

The shop girl folded her arms and stared down at Mark to assess the situation. She then caught a glance of his large, bulbous erect cock straining against his camouflage trousers as he knelt on the floor. She stepped towards him and placed the ball of her toe on his cock with one of her patent leather boots.

'Perhaps we can arrange something,' she mused. She returned to the front of the shop to turn the 'closed' sign over on the door. She returned to the cubicle at the back of the shop and began to surmise what could be done next.

The two girls stood up and vacated the cubicle, leaving Mark to stand alone and face the music.

Ava and Paris stepped away and settled down on a sofa across the room to watch the festivities.

'Well, the first thing you can do is remove your clothing,' said the shop girl. She kicked one of his boots insultingly. The shop girl stood back and smiled as she watched Mark sheepishly undress in front of her with all the embarrassment that would be expected from stripping down naked in front of a stranger. The shop girl looked him up and down, running her tongue across the front row of her teeth and licking her lips. She turned her head round to look at the girls behind her.

Without looking she reached behind her and grabbed the first thing that came to hand off a nearby rail and threw it at Mark.

'Put this on. If you want to make this a whore palace, then you can be the whore.'

She had thrown a full-length dark blue satin and lace nightgown at him. Mark slipped it over his head and stood in front of her feeling the strain of the fabric pull tight against his body. He could feel himself begin to twitch with the arousing sensation of water-silk fabric sliding over his chest, cock and thighs. The sensation gave him mixed feelings of complete vulnerability and embarrassed exposure in front of this forceful, demanding stranger who stood watching him with a serious look on her face.

'I think he'd look good on all fours on that sofa over there, don't you?' the shop girl said, with an evil smile.

Mark, still feeling ashamed of having been naked and exposed, walked over to the sofa and hunched up on all fours. The shop girl grabbed a few of the scarves from a rail and proceeded to tie his wrists and ankles to the feet of the sofa.

The two girls hopped up from the opposite sofa, giggling.

'You've got him now!' said Ava. 'We don't care what you do with him, you can do what you like with him. As long as we get to watch!'

Paris grabbed a large red, floppy hat off one of the dummy heads and put it on Mark. The shop-girl produced a dark red lipstick from her pocket and smeared it across his lips.

'Oh, you make such a pretty whore,' she said, as grabbed one of his cheeks and licked the side of his face. With that she slipped a red chiffon scarf over his eyes.

'I'll let you see a little bit, but not everything.' she added. Mark's cock flip-flopped and twitched. He knew he was now completely at the mercy of the shop girl. She pulled the blue night gown up over his back, exposing his cock and balls. It brought a sparkling, dark glint to her eyes.

'That looks fairly ... appetizing,' she commented. 'Although, I debate its functionality,' she added.

Mark piped up in his own defence 'No, it's does work. Miss, I assure you.'

'You are in no position to comment, you cheap, overly available slut-thing,' she quipped. With that said, she grabbed his cock backwards and began to haul it up between his legs.

The two girls watching began to laugh and jeer at Mark. Ava removed his blindfold and lifted a tape measure from a counter, handing it to the shop girl.

'Let's see,' she said. 'Now, do I measure from the base or from the balls? I can never decide which. Perhaps I should measure from the most prominent part of the blood flow. But then I would only need a two-inch measuring tape if that was the case.'

Mark felt a moment of deep shame as he could begin to feel the pre-cum dripping from his cock.

'Oh!' giggled Paris. 'Look at that! He's drooling all over your lovely sofa. What an inconsiderate, hussy bastard.'

'You'll pay for that, you little fucker,' the shop girl hissed. 'Two inches of cock and all this mess.'

She grabbed another scarf from the rack and tightly cinched it around his balls. Mark tried his hardest not to wince with pain. Secretly, he revelled at the thought of his cock being pinched at by the tightly tied fabric in these unfamiliar surroundings. It made him shudder with a mixture of intense pleasure and shame.

The shop girl hitched his tightly tied cock to a piece of rope that hung from the ceiling. She attached it to some pipes, then walked to the shop counter to retrieve a black magic marker.

Upon her return, she whipped round to face Mark. She shot him a huge, mocking smile, then proceeded to slide into the space between his body and the sofa. Uncapping the marker, she proceeded to write:

The words "Whore Palace Fuck Object" were scrawled across his chest in indelible marker. Then, sliding back out, she continued by writing, 'Suck my tiny cock' across his back. The two other girls howled with laughter as they watched.

Fashioning a tattoo on his arm with the marker pen, she wrote the words "2-inch cock" on his upper shoulder. She finished her artwork by drawing a batwing design across his eyes and a large smiling clown mouth over his lips.

'Should have filled that in with red pen, really.' she huffed. 'So, what is he good for now? His cock doesn't look much like it's got much to offer. Perhaps his mouth might be useful. Let's see.' Hiking up her skirt to reveal a pair of seamed stockings and orange satin suspenders, she bent over and forced her panties into Mark's face. 'Take my knickers down, slut.' she ordered. Mark began to pull the orange satin knickers down with his teeth only to find the shop girl forcing her cunt deeply against his mouth. 'Now you can lick me. But I want you to lick me better than you licked her.' I expect that extra effort for all the trouble you have caused me today. And I still might have to call the police on you if you don't make anything less than a first-class effort.'

Mark forced his tongue deep inside the girls' cunt. She writhed, using his tongue to pleasure herself as she rubbed her own clit. Ava and Paris watched on with fascination. Tears welled up in Mark's eyes with a sense of utter humiliation as she began to grind her ass into his face.

'Come here you two girls, you can help me,' said the shop girl. Ava and Paris hopped up from the sofa. 'Yes, Miss..' replied Ava and Paris in unison.

'I'd like to watch whilst you two go to work on him. You can start by tightening his restraints then perhaps you might like to engage in a little bit of cock torment.'

'With pleasure Madame,' chuckled Paris. Paris grabbed the scarf attached to Mark's balls and cinched it up tighter. She then suspended it a little bit higher from the ceiling fixing point. It began to look red and swollen. Mark felt a dull but delicious aching as his cock filled up with blood.

'Please Mistress, no, Mistress,' shouted Mark.

The shop girl folded her arms and stood back silently with an impish smile, observing the display as it began.

Ava slowly ran her long dark blue nails along the shaft of Mark's cock. Mark writhed and jumped, such was the level of sensitivity he was experiencing. Donning a pair of red leather gloves Paris found on a counter, she proceeded to slap his balls with the lightest of taps. This was all it took. More pre-cum began to drip from out of his cock in quantities that were well beyond control.

'Naughty boy,' laughed Ava.

Paris slapped him across the face. Then, as though enjoying his expression of shock, she went on to slap him five more times in succession. Each slap got harder. She watched the reddening side of his cheek begin to glow.

'You are such a dirty whore, Mark.' said Ava. 'We can hardly take you anywhere. What are you?'

'I don't know what I am Mistress Ava,' replied Mark.

Paris walked over to a large, potted rubber plant and grabbed a handful of dirt from it. She then proceeded to rub it across his face and down the length of his back. She smeared the remainder of the dirt over his cock and balls.

'You're a dirty wanker,' said Paris. 'Now repeat what I just said or I am going to get some girls from outside on the street to come in, and get a look at you like this.'

'I'm not a dirty whore Miss, I am only dirty because you have covered me in dirt, and black magic marker. You did this to me.' There was a flat tone of rebellion in his voice.

'Insolence!' howled the shop girl. 'Do you think this is all for you? Do you think this is all for your benefit? You're the one tied up here. You're the one covered in dirt having your cock tormented by two friends and a stranger. You'll come out of this exactly when we say and when we have finished doing whatever we require to do to get as much entertainment and pleasure out of you as we can devise. In fact, I think we need to demonstrate to you how dirty you are. It's obvious to everyone in the room, that you are an absolute fucking disgrace. For some reason only beknownst to you, you are not yet able to accept that. I think it's time that you came to reconcile the reality of what you really are, against your own perception of who you think you are.'

The shop-girl walked out of the shop and shut the door.

Ava and Paris stood looking at each other. Paris' eyes filled with wonder. There was an empty silence.

'I wonder where she has gone?' posed Ava.

'It's hard to say, really,' said Paris. 'Do you think we should untie him and take off?'

'I don't know,' said Ava. 'I have to admit I am curious to see what happens next. I mean, perhaps she has gone for the police.'

Mark squirmed. 'God! Please untie me, please get me out of this! I need to get out right now!'

'Yeah, perhaps we should untie him and go,' said Paris.

'Okay, you untie the arms and I will untie the legs, then we can slip out,' offered Ava.

'Oh, God thank fuck for that,' said Mark. This has just gotten all out of hand. 'If she has gone to get the police we need to get out of here.'

'I know!' exclaimed Paris.

Paris loosened the scarf that cinched his cock and balls to the ceiling.

'Wow, that's really red and swollen,' said Paris. 'Let me kiss it better,' she smiled.

'Please, let me just get out of this!' exclaimed a panicked Mark. But, before he could finish his sentence Paris has engulfed the entire length his entire swollen cock into the furthest reaches of her throat. Mark felt his cock stiffen. All thoughts that didn't involve an orgasm drained out of his mind. Ava only worsened the situation by laughing and stroking his balls.

'I wonder if I can get both of his balls in my mouth at the same time as you're sucking his cock, Miss Paris.' said Ava, as she opened her mouth wide and began to suck his balls into her warm, wet mouth. 'He doesn't taste half bad for a dirty whore,' said Paris, in-between gulps of pre-cum.

'I'm going to cum,' strained Mark.

'No, you're not.' exclaimed the shop girl as she reappeared in the doorway.

Mark looked up. Two young girls stood next to the shop girl, looking on in wonder. Kathy was about nineteen, with a short, sporty cropped bob. She was wearing a white baker's apron. Sue was also wearing a white apron, and had her hair tied up in a tight pony tail. Sue wiped her hands on her apron. Her wide eyes seemed to be out on stalks, and she stared at Mark.

'Is he a burglar?' she queried.

'No Sue. He's nothing as sophisticated as that. He's a slut.' She turned to Ava & Paris. 'Kathy and Sue work in the tea room next door. I thought they might enjoy a little education about the way a thing with a cock attached to it. They need to see how it can be easily transformed into almost anything with a minimum of effort.'

'Why is he tied up like that?' said Kathy.

'That's a very good question,' sighed Mark.

'Because he has weaknesses that are all centred around his cock, Kathy. I don't know if you know this, girls... but almost all things with cocks attached to them can be manipulated into just about any contortion, outfit or state of mind you could imagine yourself requiring them to be in. A little passing touch, a playful grab or a teasing lick... and before you know it they find themselves tied to your sofa, covered in make-up, wearing your underwear, ready to please and service you. That's really the purpose of them. Don't ever let them convince you of otherwise.'

'Can I take a photograph?' said Sue. I would quite like to upload it to my blog. The other girls I think would be very interested to know this information.

'Of course, you may,' said the shop girl. 'I am a great advocate of sharing helpful knowledge and information with other girls.' Paris and Ava looked to the two bakery girls and nodded, with a knowing smile.

Kathy stood over Mark and angled her phone at Mark. 'I'm going to film him for my friends. They are going to love this.'

'Excellent idea,' added the shop girl.

Carefully, the girls panned their phone's lenses over the length and breadth of Mark's body. Closing in on his cock and balls, they took close-up shots and laughed as they snapped away at the filthy writing across his back. To finish, they panned their camera phones across his painted face and laughed with all the spitefulness of teenage girls. Mark stared into the camera and shut his eyes with the deepest shame.

'That should be all around the village by tonight,' chortled Sue.

'But girls,' replied Ava. 'Tell your friends to never let on they know it's him when they see him in the town. Keep him guessing. This is a useful skill.'

'I guess we need to get back to work, Samantha' said Kathy.

'I'll pop over with you,' said Samantha the shop girl.

'Okay,' said Sue quizzically. 'Is there something you wanted?'

'Yes,' said Samantha as she walked over to Mark's jacket on the floor and fished out his wallet. She opened the bill fold and stripped the cash out of it. Mark shot her a look of shock.

'Be right back,' she giggled.

The three girls strode confidently out of the shop. This time with Sue and Kathy comparing photographs and giggling. Shortly after, Sam the shop girl returned with two huge light brown cardboard boxes from the tea room.

'I guess the girls are going to have to shut up shop early today, because they are all sold out of cakes now,' Ava shot Mark a big smile.

'Can we see what you've got?' enquired Paris.

Of course. Feel free to help yourself. Paris and Ava lifted the top box from the counter and stared inside. A colourful display of pink doughnuts, lemon cupcakes and iced Bakewell tarts in dozens lined out the large cardboard box. Paris ran her finger across the icing of a blue and chocolate striped doughnut and sucked the frosting.

'Mm, yum,' she said with delight. She lifted the doughnut and swiftly rubbed it over Mark's alarmed face. 'Let's give some to Mark.' Liking the idea, Ava followed suit rubbing an iced bun over Marks arse.

'Sticky buns,' Sam giggled. 'You suck his cock and I'll spank him. There must be some friction to be had with that level of stickiness.' She lifted her hand and brought it down firmly on his rump. Ava joined in, each taking turns to mercilessly beat his backside with the flat of their hands. Their faces filled with delight.

'He is sticky, isn't he? He's sticky and dirty. I'm going to lick the sugar off him,' said Ava. 'Oh, the icing is melting on his arse, it's that hot. That's a bizarre sensation to lick, wow.'

'Well I have a better idea for these cakes,' said the shop girl walking over to the counter. She again grabbed the big black marker pen and produced a large sheet of paper from under the counter. Across it she wrote "Ladies Only Saturday Sale! Free cakes with every purchase." She posted the sign up in the shop doorway.

Ava, ignoring the activity, proceeded to fellate Mark's cock.

Sam chimed 'Don't suck it too hard, just keep edging him. Keep him close but don't let his little firework go off just yet.'

'Why is that?' said Paris.

'Because I think he should have the audience he seemed so much to crave earlier this afternoon. That should be happening in due course.

For the next forty-five minutes, the bell of the shop door clanged, spilling in a succession of young girls, middle-aged women and even a few older ladies in search of free cake and a pleasant surprise.

Samantha directed them one-by-one to the back of the shop. Each time another woman poked their head through the door to view the scene, another raucous roar of laughter emitted from the back of the shop. It was accompanied by comments such as 'What's going on back here, then?'

Only once did an older lady peep into the back room with complete disdain and announce. 'He's absolutely disgusting!' On that, she turned heel and walked out of the shop.

"Use Me" was soon scrawled across a spare patch in black magic marker on Mark's back. No one owned up to having written it, but everyone seemed amicable to the idea.

More cake was smeared across Mark's face and kissed off. Random women smiled and laughed, pulling apart his arse cheeks and commenting on the pinkness of his arsehole, slapping and smacking his cock, updating his lipstick and making observances and comments of the level of cum that seemed to slip endlessly from out of the top of his penis.

'Have you tasted it?' said one girl to another. 'It tastes a bit salty.' Then, treating his cock much like a spigot, the girls proceeded to let it drip onto the tops of their cupcakes, whilst looking him straight in the eye. With enormous, evil smiles as they each polished off their snacks.

'Dirty Slut' laughed one of the girls.

'What shall we do with him now?' said Ava.

'Well, my boots need a good clean,' said Paris. 'In fact, everything of mine needs a good clean. My boots, my stockings and even my toes.'

'Yes, my shoes need a shine,' chimed in one of the visiting ladies.

'Oh, I'd like that too,' added another.

Mark was duly untied and his clothes were hidden. A woman shoved her boot into Mark's face. 'Make it shiny,' said the woman. 'Make it shiny with your tongue.' Mark licked the length of her ankle boot from heel-to-toe. She raised the sole and beckoned his tongue again. Make it shiny everywhere, boy.' As she looked down at him, a sparkle grew in her eyes. She towered over him, forcing the sole of her shoe into his mouth. Another lady stepped forward. She was a plump, pretty, shy looking Indian lady in her late thirties with very long black hair. Gingerly, she approached him and stood gazing down at him.

'I have never done anything like this but I have always wanted to,' she exclaimed as she lifted her skirt and planted her arse firmly on Mark's face. The force of her weight knocked Mark to the floor.

The other ladies clapped and cheered. The woman parted her pussy lips and began to wriggle on Mark's face.

'Thank you, Mistress,' said Mark in between her groans.

'Suck my clit, service me correctly,' she directed. 'I like how you call me Mistress. I always wanted to be my husband's Mistress but he didn't understand this. He has no idea how to please me. Perhaps I should film this and show him what I really want.'

'Yes,' said Ava. 'I think you should show all your husbands and boyfriends what they should be doing tonight.'

A plethora of women produced mobile phones from their handbags and began snapping and filming the scene.

'I think my husband will be very angry at you for what you've done to me when I show him this tonight. I think you will have to be very careful in the town and watch out that my husband doesn't decide to sneak up behind you sometime,' said the pretty Indian lady.

'Please don't show that to him, Mistress,' pleaded Mark.

The pretty woman stood up from Mark and began to drag and whip her hair along his body like a switch. Mark could feel his cock aching with denial as the gang of women studied him intently.

'Well, perhaps we could work something out, perhaps for a while I can be your Mistress and you can service me the way I require, then I won't show my extremely volatile husband what you've been doing with me in this film on my phone.'

'I'll give you Mark's number,' said Paris.

Mark's mind raced. He thought about the different consequences of his options. On one hand, he would be at the beck and call of a stranger who would use and experiment with him as his Mistress.

There was every possibility that that scenario may end up with her husband arriving home, and discovering the two mid-sex session. He imagined the man grabbing a large knife from the kitchen and chasing him down the street naked, with every intention of maiming Mark for the violation of his wife. On the other hand, his other choice would be to refuse, and have this same woman showing her husband the sordid picture of him, in a blue satin nightgown, covered in filth with this man's wife wriggling on his face. This could also mean her volatile husband could be pounding the streets looking for Mark by the end of the night. He decided it best to choose the lesser of two evils.

'Yes,' said 'Mark, I will be your servant if you promise not to show your husband the film.'

Mark felt defeated. He thought back to more peaceful days when he used to just chat up girls, take them out for a few drinks and be satisfied with a quick romp and some vanilla sex back at the girls' flat. When he first met Paris and she had intimated to him that she had a desire to have a threesome, he was only too happy to jump at the chance. They started meeting up regularly with Ava shortly after that.

There were times when he didn't fully understand his role in their three-way liaison. Sometimes the two girls would seem more engrossed in each other when they were romping together. For hours at a time, they would be caress and worship each other; leaving him just to watch. When that happened, he felt literally like a spare cock at an orgy.

On some evenings, Paris and Ava would dress up in sheer black or baby pink lingerie and fluffy heels. They would spend hours dancing together sexually in the living room. At first, he thought it was for his benefit, but he soon grew uncertain about that belief. One time, they got him to agree to be tied up so he could watch whilst they performed lap dances for him. Before long, it descended into a full girl on girl fuck session with strap-on dildos. All that Mark was allowed to do, was watch. After a while, they blindfolded him. It was even more torturous, as he listened to the moaning and grunting of the women during orgasm after orgasm, without being allowed to join in. In fact, he'd also noticed that these women hardly ever let him cum. They seemed intent on edging him to the very brink of orgasm and only to find a new excuse for preventing his climax. He could count the times on one hand when Paris had made the concerted effort to drain every drop of cum out of his balls. He remembered she took days and days of teasing him to get to that point. He reminisced about the immense pain and frustration she had inflicted on him with her constant barrage of sexual actions and activities she had made him experience. Each time there had been the promise of an ever-impending, mind-blowing trip that would culminate in him shooting his load in technicolour. For days, sometimes weeks, Paris would take him to all sorts of locations, the seaside, clubs, fancy hotels, even Tower Bridge late at night, or web-camming in front of her girlfriends, parks, car parks or dogging sites… She always dressed in lingerie or hard black leather, always dipping deep into the darkest part of his subconscious trying to force his mind into a psyche that promised the most violent of orgasms from him. Yet, she rarely let him get there. And when he did cum, it was randomly taken from him when he was least expecting it. The last orgasm he had had, was in a church on the back pew. It might have been more pleasurable if there had not been a funeral of some complete strangers going on at the other end of the church. Paris seemed to take every delight in uncomfortable, distracting situations with him. She would wait until someone got just close enough to where they were sitting in the secluded part of the church, then reach over, discreetly starting to wank and suck his cock. The force of her sucking made it impossible for him to be able to stop her. She seemed to have so much power and control over the intensity, exact time and date of his next orgasm. It was like there was a calendar or schedule for his next appointment with sex but it was not information he was in the slightest bit privy to. The only time that she ever seemed to want to let him cum, was when he was when his heart was practically in his mouth with embarrassment and fear. He had a tough time understanding Paris' motivations, and why this all gave her so much pleasure. He also found the game impossible to resist. He was addicted to her sexual whims.

And Ava, Ava was just as bad. There was something about Ava that had served to corrupt Paris even more. Very often, Mark felt as though Ava was just there for Paris, and not for them both. Her detrimental verbal cruelty towards Mark always perplexed him, yet she also took the utmost care in mounting and teasing him for the benefit of Paris's viewing pleasure. This happened on a regular basis. He felt that Ava *must* have liked him to want to spend so much time embedded on his cock, yet at the same time she had this way of talking down to him like he was just a piece of meat. She also spent an inordinate amount of time on the phone to Paris. Mark would frequently find himself flipping through the television channels feeling marginalised, as he listened to the two girls flirting and giggling over the phone. They seemed to plot their little plans in hushed tones whilst making sure Mark could hear only the odd choice word. Their diabolical bursts of laughter drove his mind into a tailspin wondering what was being planned, or if any part of their conversation was about him. When Ava came to visit, she used to come in and check Mark over. She would survey and grab at him like a piece of livestock. Paris and Ava would chat about Mark as though he wasn't there. His clothes would be wrapped and unwrapped. His cock commented on, his last sexual performance recounted to Ava and rated fully out of ten, judging his visual and sensual properties coupled with a commentary on his recent ability, force and efficacy. Three-way phone conversations were set up with an unknown third party to recount every intimate sexual detail, which they would share in a lively fashion with their mysterious friend. Ava loved to shoot Mark a diabolical smile when they did these things. Because of it, her smile was burned permanently into his mind.

'You're going to get an amazing surprise tonight, Mark,' Ava once said, leading him on. Nothing happened. Mark spent the whole night lying in bed wondering what was and when this surprise was going to come. The next time he saw her, he asked her what the surprise was supposed to have been.

'Oh, you are a poor little cock-driven idiot,' said Ava, laughing dismissively. Paris and Ava then hugged and wiped away tears of laughter and made him watch as they shared a passionate French kiss.

Mark quickly broke out of his trance. He realised had been staring at Ava for some time.

'Your cock is too hard now. I think we should start from scratch,' said the shop girl as she tipped a jug of ice water over his lower torso. Mark shrieked sharply, and felt the immediate dulling of his erection as it died away from the shock of the freezing-cold ice water.

'Sadly, there is no amount of water that will ever make him clean,' said Ava. 'He's been a readily available, dirty slut to all from the get-go. No matter how hard we have tried to correct him, he always seems to end up in these sorts of predicaments. He's quite transparent, really. I am tempted to just drop him off here and leave you girls to it.'

The shop girl piped up. 'I know, let's hold a charity fuck auction for him. The highest bidder gets to take him home for the next 3 days and do whatever she likes with him. We can give the money to the cat's protection home. I'll even drop him off with the winner from the boot of my car.'

What proceeded to commence, was the most unusual of bidding wars.

'I bid, one hundred and fifty pounds!' shouted one woman.

'Five hundred!' shouted another.

'Two pounds and twenty-five pence!' shouted another. 'And he's hardly worth it at that!'

Laughter erupted around the room.

'I bid two tins of baked beans and a chocolate bar,' laughed Paris.

'I'll trade his watch!' laughed Ava.

'Hey, that's my watch!' shouted Mark, as Ava ripped it off if his wrist. 'That's a Breitling watch!'

Ava burst out laughing.

'Well, I think I win then. There's a lot of little happy kitties going to be snuggling up nicely thanks to your slutdom. We can sell this online and help far more worthy creatures than you, now. Think of it that way. I guess you'll just have to get your ass out there and work for another watch, won't you? That's the price of being a slut.'

'Sold!' shouted the shop girl.

The female audience clapped politely.

'Have you got any bubble wrap?' giggled Paris.

'Yes,' said Samantha. 'I'll wrap him up for you.' Shortly thereafter, Mark found himself being tightly wrapped in bubble wrap. Sam sealed him up with parcel tape. She used a wide length of purple satin ribbon to tie a bow around his waist. A bigger bow was festooned over his cock. From the back room, she produced a trolley and bumped Mark into place on it.

'I think I'll bring the car round,' said Paris.

The large group of women began to usher out of the shop, reviewing their little films and chatting excitedly about the day's events as they left.

The two girls prepared to leave, wheeling the marker-covered, bubble wrapped. deflated shell of the man that was Paris' & Ava's now fully worked-over slave.

'Thanks, Sam, for letting us use the shop,' said Ava. 'Nice to see you again.' They hugged.

'Yeah, no worries,' replied Sam, as she returned to pricing a pile of jewellery on the counter. 'See you soon,' said Sam. The two girls departed, pushing the trolley of goods.

BITE

Ava settled down in her seat on the Intercity train back to London. She felt satisfied with her recent exciting foray into the world of lascivious slave torment and subjugation. She glanced at her mobile phone and delighted at the collection of pictures and video footage she had taken of him throughout the previous day as he had been forced by her to dress in a satin nightgown. He had had his balls suspended from the ceiling of a strange boutique and was subsequently ridiculed and objectified by a gang of at least twenty-five women. She couldn't stop laughing at the thought of all those girls teasing and deriding him simultaneously.

'What a day,' she thought. She closed her eyes and savoured the last part of it as dusk settled. It had involved watching her friend Paris ride their slave, Mark, like a bucking bronco whilst he was still encased in bubble wrap. She *did* feel Mark was totally deserving of that level of objectification. It was Ava's view that if a brain surgeon were to operate on Mark's brain (for some reason) he would probably just find another cock in there. She also knew in truth, that Mark adored being the centre of their sexual attentions.

Mark wasn't the kind of man you would be discussing art and playing chess with, that was for sure. To Ava, he was mostly a lump of male gristle that they used and abused purely to release sexual tension. She had told that to Mark's face on many occasions, and usually when he had a gag in place. But she knew telling him that made also him extremely happy. Because she often noticed that he gave away a little subconscious nod of admission.

One time they dressed him up in evening gear and made him take them into London for a night out. The girls laughed as he showed up at his favourite restaurant like Charlie big bollocks, trying to show off with a beautiful girl on each arm. Paris and Ava would wear slinky black dresses, stockings, black lace lingerie, very high heels and sported matching little designer handbags. What his friends and associates didn't know, were the same facts that always kept Paris and Ava thoroughly entertained. Mark had ridden all the way to the London restaurant in the boot of their car. The two girls sat in the front seat, singing along to the radio, giggling at Mark as they listened to him pound his fists on the roof of the trunk.

'Shut up back there, you whore! Or I'll order the worst dinner for you that I can think of!' laughed Paris.

The boot clunked again. Mark yelled with a bit of urgency.

'Mistresses!' shouted Mark.

'Oh God,' huffed Ava. 'What now? We had better pull into a lay-by.'

Paris changed down a gear and found a dark lay-by that looked quiet. The two girls hopped out of the front seat and opened the boot of the car to survey what was going on with Mark.

'Mistresses! Can I not ride in the back seat of the car?' Mark said tearfully.

'I'll tell you what,' said Ava. 'You can ride in the back seat but we will have to gaffer tape your cock to your belly button and you will have to spend the rest of the night like that.' Paris grabbed Mark's exposed cock and began to play with it. 'Or you can stay back here and be nice and quiet and continue to play with yourself until you go blind,' said a mocking Paris. 'It's your choice.'

Mark felt a breeze wash over him, the discomfort of the bondage in the boot of the car began to fade away as he watched the two girls begin to reach in. They started again trying to edge his cock to the point of orgasm. Ava grabbed the head of his cock and began to force her tongue down the eye of it.

'Now, does that feel better?' she teased.

'I … guess I … will stay … back here and … be nice,' said Mark.

' .. and quiet,' Paris said, finishing his sentence. Ava produced a roll of gaffer tape and placed it over Mark's mouth. With sparkling smiles, the two girls shut the trunk of the car and returned to speeding down the dark motorway into the night, headed for London. They resumed singing along to music from the radio from top of their lungs, ignoring their hapless cargo.

As they arrived in London the girls headed for a quiet car park on the edges of Central London. It was one that they well and had parked in before. It was beside the centre of town, but was classed more as Holborn, which was just east of Soho. Occasionally, they would dare to park right in the centre of Soho and fish Mark publicly out of the boot. They found the gay district of Soho to be a lot more open-minded about kinky play at night and liked to enjoy those liberties. In other parts of Soho, especially at the weekend, they had noticed no one cared what they got up to after dark. On this occasion, they felt inclined for this event to keep their plans more discreet.

They parked on the top floor of the concrete car park and lifted the door of the boot again. Ava ripped the gaffer tape from Mark's mouth brusquely.

'Now are we going to be a good boy tonight?' demanded Ava. 'No staring, no tongues hanging out at other ladies. No humping legs and such. We're going to be an obedient dog, aren't we? Or you'll have to stay in the car. Promise now.'

'Yes, Mistresses,' replied Mark.

'You know Ava,' mused Paris. 'I see a little bit of lying in his eyes. I can't say I fully trust him to behave this evening. I get the feeling that he's either going to try to misbehave, in order to gain attention, or try to take control of the situation tonight. What do you think?'

'I think you're quite right, Madame,' said Ava fondly. 'We should get the picnic basket out.'

Paris produced a perfect, leather-trimmed wicker picnic basket from the back seat of the car. She opened it to reveal a stunning array of different bondage items. They glittered like jewels. Inside was a roll of cling film, a latex hood, a gas mask, a shiny silver chain, a red rope and all sorts of other interesting tools of correction. They were all neatly organised inside of the basket. The two women studied the contents, trying to decide which item would best serve their needs for their dinner outing. Paris lifted a remote control electric massager.

'This!' she squealed. 'This will keep us entertained! We could gaffer tape it to his cock.'

'No,' said a serious Ava, 'I have better plans for his cock tonight. Although, there's no reason why we can't smuggle this somewhere else into his person.'

'No Mistresses, please don't!' Mark pulled a face of pure horror. In truth, it masked a deep satisfaction from the gross level of pleasure he was receiving via the studied actions of two cruel, but beautiful women. Mark adored their attentions.

Paris ripped Mark's shirt up around to just beneath his chest. Ava equally pulled his pants down to his knees as he wriggled around in the boot of the car being his usual, difficult self. Ava flipped him over forcefully and inserted the remote-controlled vibrating bullet into Mark's newly exposed arse.

'Now we need something to keep that in place,' she said with a concentrated frown. Paris lifted a black leather device with bondage straps from the picnic basket.

'Well, we could use this if we modified it a little bit. Perhaps we could remove the arm restraints,' chimed Paris. She set about stripping out the arm restraints that would have held Mark's arms to his sides and held up the rest of the leather body cage. It was never in either of the girl's interests when to draw any attention to themselves when they went out in the busy West End. They both usually got some very flirtatious looks, but beyond that they just wanted to be left in peace to play the games they had planned. The main goal for the evening's entertainment was to attain a level of pleasure that would equal their slave's torment. They both felt that if they could achieve this state, a successful night out would be had by all, (apart from the slave.) His pleasure was insignificant to them.

'We will untie you in a minute. We just have to make some minor adjustments,' said Ava. She watched as Paris cinched the black leather strap around Mark's waist, bringing the device down between his legs. She used the cage to strap the vibrating bullet they had placed up his arse into position. She then fastened the body cage over Mark's exposed cock and balls, pulling them through fitted gap that was especially worked into the black leather for that purpose.

'That should hold it,' said Paris.

'Yes Paris, that will work very well,' she replied. 'But let's make sure we don't have any nonsense from him tonight for certain.' Ava lifted a metal chastity device from the basket. She also picked up a pair of metal-chained nipple clamps with added sail clips. She began to force the length of Mark's bulging cock down inside of the spiked bars of the cage. She then fitted a padlock at the base of his balls. Ava then strung the chain of the nipple clamps under one of the bars of the chastity device and proceeded to lace the two sail clips up to firmly plant them on his nipples. Standing over Mark, she smiled. She began to carefully close the nipple clamps, one at a time onto each nipple. She did this very slowly, in order cut off the blood supply. The operative term here was not pain, but discomfort. Mark's body was now tightly cinched up and padlocked with the added nuance of a remotely controlled electrocution device concealed within his person. Mark thought about the situation dolefully. He knew that the two women now had him exactly where they wanted him for the rest of the evening. He sighed. For good measure, Ava pulled a strip of gaffer tape from a roll in the basket, and sealed it across his buttocks.

Paris then readjusted up Mark's shirt and trousers, to conceal his bondage from the public.

'There, good as gold, good to go. Now, let's go have dinner,' said Paris. The two girls bodily heaved Mark out of the boot of the car.

Mark hobbled to his feet unsteadily. Paris handed the remote-control device to Ava.

'You go first. In fact, let's have some fun with it. We should let him lead the way to the restaurant, and if he goes in the wrong direction- we zap him!' said Paris.

'Okay, Mistresses,' said Mark. 'but I don't know where I am supposed to be going.'

'Well, we will give you a clue. It's a blue fronted building. They specialise in seafood,' remarked Paris. 'That's your one clue.'

Mark smiled. He knew exactly which restaurant they were booked in to. It was their favourite. Mark had an extremely naughty nature and a lot of physical vigour. It meant to him that he knew he could take quite a few shocks from his Mistresses in return for running them around on a wild goose chase first. He smiled to himself, knowing that those high heels of theirs would be very sore by the time they got to the restaurant, due to the meandering route he intended to take them on.

Mark jumped into action and ran half way up the street. He knew if he could get out of range, then girls would be too far away to zap him. Paris and Ava shouted at him and gave chase, zapping furiously. The electrified egg radiating in his ass was very shocking. It made him want to cum, jump and scream all at the same time. He attempted running as far ahead of them as he could, in order to get as far away from the remote-control device's range as he could manage. He turned a corner into a dark alleyway beside a theatre and hid in the backstage doorway. He steadied and silenced his breathing, as he listened out for them. He soon heard the sharp clacking of two pairs of high heels as they entered the passageway.

'Oh, that little trollop! He's going to make us miss our table!' fumed Ava.

'Shh,' said Paris. 'Wait a minute. Perhaps he didn't come this way,' she said winking at Ava.

Ava smiled back. 'No, I think he went down into the other alleyway. Let's go check that one out.'

Mark breathed a sigh of relief as he watched the two girls exit the passageway. He knew that if they walked to the end of this street, he would have a chance to slip away. Then they would have to spend their night hunting for him around Soho. The two girls crept into the opposite passage. Quietly, they both removed their high heels and padded stealthily up behind him.

Ava pressed her finger hard down on the remote-control device with a loud zap.

'Aaargh!' shouted Mark.

'This is no less than I expected from you!' zapped Ava five more times. 'Now get in front of us. No running. No more hide and seek. If you want anyone or anything apart from a pair of pliers to ever touch your cock again, you are going to behave tonight!' directed a stern Ava.

Mark stifled a giggle. He knew of he had one up on the two girls. He could outrun them both. But, he decided to play it straight for a little while. He knew he could have a little more fun tormenting them a bit later.

The three walked on into the neon, noise and bustle of the red-light district of Soho.

'You know,' said Paris. 'We never learned how to enjoy life like this this at that ladies' auxiliary union tea party we went to last month. This is a damn sight more fun.'

'I know!' said Ava. 'All that baking cakes and macramé and such. What was that all for? It was a bloody waste of time! I am ten times more interested in getting that thing over there trained into submission. Fuck macramé!'

The two girls laughed as they arrived at the door of the restaurant.

'Table for three?' said the waitress.

'Well, two and a high chair,' said Ava. The waitress smiled. She showed them to a four-seater table.

The waitress handed out the menus.

'Can I show you the specials?'

Ava confiscated Mark's menu and browsed over the drinks list. She pointed to one of the wines on the list. 'May we have a bottle of the prosecco, please?' The waitress walked from the table returning with three champagne flutes. She began to pour out the wine.

The waitress left the table. Mark raised his glass.

'Cheers, ladies,' he said boldly. He downed his glass of wine. Paris pressed the remote-control device with a silent zap. The glass shook as Mark shook.

The light danced in the two girl's eyes with frivolity as they watched his torture.

'You did lead us a merry dance to this restaurant Mark, do you not remember? We have not forgotten your recent misdemeanour,' posed Paris. 'In fact,' she said, swiping his prosecco 'Let me freshen up your wine.' Paris lifted the salt and began to dump it into the glass. It made a slight fizzing noise. Ava joined in, adding pepper from a selection of condiments on the table. 'That's much better,' Paris said. 'Now let's have a look at the menu and see what Mark is going to have for dinner.' The girls perused the menu and called the waitress over.

'May I have the sea bass with cherries please? That sounds delicious,' Ava said politely to the waitress.

'I'll have the Cornish crab,' added Paris. Mark will have the white bait. That will be perfect for him.'

Mark frowned. The girls were knowledgeable to the fact that he didn't like white bait. It was a horrible, sardine-like taste. The dozens of little frowning mouths that would be staring up at him from the plate. The added horror of their crunchy little heads didn't make his dinner prospects any more appetizing to him at that. He knew they had ordered it simply to observe his expression of disgust over the dinner table.

Paris looked over Mark dismissively. 'He looks like he could do with a trip to the ladies' room really,' she said with a dark glint in her eye.

Ava smiled. She reached over as though to kiss Mark on the lips. Instead, she discreetly snatched at a nipple clamp through the fabric of his shirt.

'Off we go!' she said. Mark felt himself being lifted from the table in the busy restaurant by one of his nipple clamps.

The two darted quickly towards the ladies' room. Ava jostled him into an empty cubicle.

'Now let's see how you are getting on,' said Ava with a studying frown. 'It's best you don't speak. You might get thrown out of this restaurant for being in the ladies' room. They take a dim view of that in this establishment.'

Ava unzipped the flies of Marks trousers, revealing the shiny silver chastity device. With amusement she knelt over it, teasing it with her tongue. Her tongue darted between the silver bars of the device, licking the skin of Mark's trapped prick. Mark could feel his cock tightening in the chastity cage. The pressure he felt was extremely uncomfortable. Ava looked at his contraption hungrily, calculating what the best option would be to take. She wanted extract as much of an internal struggle as she could imagine from the her aroused, but hapless servant.

'You can lick me, but don't tell Paris when we go back to the table. Kneel down and lick me,' ordered Ava.

'Yes Mistress,' Mark complied.

Ava moaned in the cubicle for the next five minutes as Mark buried his tongue deep into her cunt. She felt herself getting to the edge of orgasm. But felt a little bit of a nagging problem in her mind that there wasn't enough excitement going on from Mark's efforts to quite get her there. She pushed Mark away with an expression of disdain towards him. She lifted her mobile phone out of her purse and dialled Paris's number. Paris answered and listened on intently as Ava pushed Mark's head back into her pussy and carried on moaning. Mark resumed sucking on Ava's pussy as ordered. After a few more minutes, Paris entered the ladies room.

'This little whore of yours is not getting me off,' said a disgruntled Ava.

'Let's get him into the men's toilet, and disgrace him there,' Paris concluded.

'No, I have a better idea,' said Ava. 'You watch him. Make sure he doesn't do anything untoward. I'll be right back.'

Ava darted out of the toilet. She shortly returned with a quiet-looking, bespectacled, middle-aged man. She had been outside the ladies' room and had quickly spotted him as was exiting the men's toilet. She had grabbed him by his tie and dragged him into the ladies. He had been too confused to protest.

Ava turned to the man and lifted her skirt to reveal her shaved pussy. 'Do you like this?' she said to the man.

'Yes,' he replied in a flustered tone. 'Well, good,' she said, bending over the sink. 'So, you can show that no-hoper over there how to make a girl cum, can't you?'

Ava lifted her skirt and grabbed the man roughly. Within a minute the stranger's cock was buried deep inside her cunt. Mark looked on, watching hopelessly as the two grunted and fucked against the sink of the ladies' room. Ava could feel the release of her orgasm rush to her brain. Paris turned to the man and sat spread-legged across the sink. She started to finger her wet pussy for him. Ava pulled her tits out of her bra and began to fondle them in an attempt to egg the man on.

'It's my turn. Fuck me as well,' said Paris. That no-dick sissy never knows how to show us a good fuck. The man had an instant erection again. Hynotically, the man pushed his cock deeply into the second girl's cunt as Mark watched. Paris stared into Mark's eyes, knowing the scene would make him feel totally useless. She knew that the sight of watching a stranger enter and satisfy both of the women that he was supposed to be chaperoning, would be completely humiliating to him. At the same time, it was a complete turn-on. The added misery for Mark was the fact that he couldn't play with his cock as he watched them. It made the watching of the entire spectacle, highly punishing to him.

Paris could feel her cunt aching. The sensation of fucking a random person in front of her boyfriend was something she found incredibly arousing.

'When I do cum, Mark. I hope you will be taking notes. Because it's something you are completely incompetent at. And we might have to opt for this new man as our new boyfriend instead of you, if you don't improve your skills.'

This only served to make the random stranger ride her harder. Ava grabbed at and sucked Paris's nipples. Ava could feel the tingling that was telling her that she was about to come. It turned out to be timed exactly to a moment when another woman walked into the ladies' room.

Looking a bit shocked, the woman attempted to exit as quickly as she entered. But the door opened quietly again. The woman stared in, transfixed at the scene.

'Would you like to see the specials?' chuckled Ava. 'Come in, come in. It's okay.'

The young girl was about twenty-five and of eastern European extraction. She looked over at the cage that engulfed their slave's cock.

'Can I look at that?' she asked, innocently.

'He's there for your use if you like,' snuffed Paris. 'He costs fifty pence a shot.'

'What will he do for fifty pence?' said the woman with a little laugh.

'Anything you like as long as it doesn't take too long, because our dinner is coming soon,' laughed Ava.

'I'll do anything for twenty-five pence,' said the middle-aged man.

'Oh, get out!' laughed Paris hurling him out of the door. 'This is the ladies room!'

'Now back to you,' said Paris to the girl. 'What would you like, sweetie? You can have anything you want.'

'Well, I came in to go for a pee. Perhaps, I could use your man instead?'

'Okay. But we need the fifty pence first,' chuckled Ava.

The girl politely produced a shiny silver fifty pence piece. She handed it over to the girls timidly.

Ava and Paris wrangled Mark back into one of the toilet cubicles. They made him kneel.

Paris put her heel briefly on Mark's cock.

'Behave Mark. Be nice, and you'll get treats later if you do.'

The twenty-five-year old girl curiously entered the cubicle. She looked back at the two women. They nodded with a little smile of approval as she entered the tiny room. Mark knelt before the strange girl, with a humbled look of submission. He looked up at her and opened his mouth. The girl shyly lifted her skirt and planted her pussy over Mark's face. He soon could feel his mouth filling up with warm piss. Ava banged on the door.

'Don't forget to swallow!' she laughed. 'Or you may well drown!'

With a hard gulp, he could feel the hot yellow pungent water stream into the back of his throat. Growing more confident, the girl began to force the stream harder into his mouth.

'Drink it,' she whispered shyly. 'Drink it, you dirty boy.'

With all pee now emptied out of the girl. Mark sucked the tiny crevice of the girl's pussy until it was clean. She moaned with delight. Then remembering herself, she straightened up and left the cubicle.

'He's such a whore,' said Ava. The woman stood at the sink, washing her hands. 'We can't take him anywhere. But thank you for your custom. Come again soon!'

'I suppose we should get back to the food,' said Ava. 'Mark, you come back to the table in a few minutes. That way no one will catch on.'

Mark nodded. By this point, he hardly felt hungry any more. The humiliation of drinking the piss of an unknown person at the behest of the two evil bitches (that he found himself addicted to the company of) had thoroughly made him lose his appetite.

The girls exited the ladies room and settled themselves back at their spot in the restaurant. Mark's plate of white bait was ready and steaming at the table.

'Oh waitress? May we have some hot English mustard, cranberry sauce and possibly some hot fudge sauce as well, please? I have a medical condition,' said Paris. She made a deadpan serious expression.

The waitress looked bemused and returned shortly with the ordered items. The waitress made no comments as she witnessed the two girls dowsing Mark's whitebait with a colourful array of uncomplimentary sauces. Mark returned to the table and sat down in front of his plate. The two women jovially ate their delicious dinner.

'Not eating Mark? We expect you to finish your dinner. This is a very exclusive restaurant, you know. The chef has been known to take offence.'

Mark winced at the sight. Not only was it a dish that he couldn't stand, but it was also laden with a ramshackle combination of condiments. They had sabotaged him. He lifted the fork and began to move the fish around the plate. Paris firmly planted the button down again on the remote-control device with a succession of fourteen zaps. By the fourteenth Zap Mark decided perhaps he should just eat it and get it over with, all the while plotting his revenge against the ladies.

Deciding to show no reaction whatsoever. Mark finished his plate in a short sitting. The girls started out by laughing at his distress, but this soon turned to dismay to find that he wasn't as disgusted as they had hoped he would be.

'Lovely,' smiled Mark as he downed a glass of salty prosecco.

Ava frowned. 'We have hardened that little prick off too much now.' Ava covertly sent a text to Paris as she sat next to her at the dinner table.

'He's not reacting to anything we do to him,' Paris texted. 'This makes him an unknown quantity. We are going to have to play hard ball with him.'

Paris turned to Ava and nodded. 'Let's get the bill and get him out of here.'

Mark lifted his hand to summon the waitress. 'May we have the bill please?' he asked sweetly. He watched the two women, surmising that they were intently planning another plot against him.

'If these girls want my submission they are going to have to work for it tonight,' he thought.

The waitress arrived at the table.

'Tell the waitress what you are wearing under your clothes and what you ate and drank tonight, Mark,' said Ava. She kicked him hard in the shin under the table.

Mark turned to the waitress. 'Underneath my clothing I am wearing a system of electrified anal cock torment devices and these ladies made me drink one of your client's piss in the ladies' room earlier in the evening.' The waitress looked at him with shocked surprise. She shot him a nonplussed smile.

'Mark is our slut, Madame,' said Ava. 'And to apologise for his heinous presence at your place of work he is going to tip you double the price of the entire meal this evening, aren't you Mark?' Mark rubbed his eyes and face. He put his head in his hands.

'Yes, I suppose so,' he added ruefully.

'Thank you, Ladies,' chirped the waitress. 'You are a funny table, tonight.'

The trio got up to leave the noisy dining hall. Foolishly, Paris left her handbag open. It was open just enough for Mark to spot the fob that held not only his chastity device key, but also the car keys. Surreptitiously, he lifted both sets of keys without Paris or Ava noticing. The three walked out onto the pavement and began to make their way back to the car.

'That was a horrible dinner,' stated Mark.

'You say that Mark… but you know we are going to ride you like the first horse out of the gate at Kempton Park Racecourse when we get home, because you have entertained us so much. So, quit moaning!' teased Ava.

The two girls clacked along the Soho street a few paces in front of Mark. Their gate was very triumphant. The girls stopped to admire a small shop window display. It was decorated with a colourful collection of sequinned carnival costumes. With great subtlety, Mark slowed his gait down behind them. He then darted off, disappearing into the back streets of Soho. He felt a rush of adrenaline from the knowledge that he had finally managed to give the girls the slip. He made sure he was at least, a good quarter of a mile away before dashing into the men's room of a local pub. Inside, he began to unlock and disentangle his body from the complicated system of leather straps coupled with the electrified anal butt plug that had served to tormented him for the whole evening. He decided that it was his turn for revenge. He wanted to get them both back for the way they had ruined his evening. He removed the padlock from his cock and eased the chastity device from it, carefully avoiding the spikes. His cock stood fully to attention. He found himself aching for an orgasm, but resolved that is was the job of those two little bitches to take care of that later. He loved them both, but he still wanted a little revenge. He left the pub and sauntered back to the car. Now relaxed, he sprawled across the back seat listening to the radio. He waited enthusiastically for their return, looking forward to their reaction when they both realised they were locked out of their own car.

After much searching around Soho for Mark to no avail, Ava and Paris were now exasperated. They returned to the car.

'Let's make him walk home, in his bondage,' said Paris. She began to hunt through her handbag for the car keys.

'I can't find them!' she exclaimed. After a moment, Mark sat up in the back seat of the car dangling their keys. The girls looked at him with faces full of fury. Their eyes filled with a cruel, breathtakingly sexy rage.

'Well, I will be happy to trade you the keys in return for your clothes, ladies,' quipped Mark. He let the window down by a tiny crack. Just slip them through here. Then I will let you have the keys.

'Mark!' shouted Paris. 'I am not getting naked in the middle of a car park!'

Mark slid to the front seat of the car and turned on the ignition.

'Okay, as you wish. I'll see you back at the house,' he joshed.

'No!' shouted Ava. 'I really don't care if I have to go home naked. As long as I don't have to deal with wandering around London looking for a train.' Ava began to strip down to her seamed stockings and suspenders which were matched by a blood red bra and pair of panties. Paris soon followed. They fed their clothing to Mark through the tiny crack in the car window.

'I did say everything girls, but you can keep your stockings, suspenders and heels on,' he shot them a wicked, self-satisfied smile.

The two girls were now furious but in no other position but to comply. They slotted the last of their requested clothing through the crack in the window. Mark licked his lips as he saw his two Mistresses standing naked and helpless in front of him. It was a delicious sight, but he knew he was going to get into terrible trouble for it at some point in the future. Right now, he was the dominant and they were the submissives. He decided that he wanted to savour that fact for a few moments longer. He lifted the chastity cage and dangled it in front of them.

'I guess trying to zap me has not been working much lately on the way back to the car, I gather?' he chortled. 'I've ditched those keys, and we are not going anywhere until you agree that I have been a good gentleman all night and that I indeed, deserve a reward. You can now address me as "Master". After all, look at where you are... and look at where I am.'

The girls looked at him with fury. Ava stamped her heel. He rolled the window down.

'I think each of you should present your bottoms for a spanking. Then I expect a full servicing to my cock. I expect you to swallow, as well.'

Ava was first to present her naked bottom to the car window. She shut her eyes and faced away from the car as Mark brought down blow after blow of the spanking upon her round arse cheeks. Her bottom turned bright red. Paris's punishment followed in tandem. The two girls, naked and now with sore, spanked, bright red bottoms leant into the car window and took turns sucking Marks previously, extremely frustrated cock. The sight of the two naked girls servicing him with the relative danger of discovery in this lonely central London car park was a huge rush for him. He felt like he might want to explode with the backlog of spunk he had amassed, from their previous weeks of sexual denial. The pressure from having been made to wait so long before he could cum had made his prick feel like it was part of a reactor melting down. He held Paris's head tightly in place as he shot his load straight onto her tongue. Now spent, he unlocked the car and let the girls in.

'Good girls,' he said condescendingly. The two girls sat in the back seat looking disgruntled. The both began to put their clothes back on. Ava quietly spied the picnic basket on the floor of the back seat. She winked at Paris.

She spotted a pair of standard handcuffs, and lifted them out of the basket as silently as she could. Leaping into the front seat, Paris barrelled towards Mark and grabbed his hands. Ava, with the speed of a leopard quickly handcuffed Mark's wrists to the steering wheel. Now, not feeling so much angry but resigned, Mark had a good idea of what was to come next.

'Now *you* can drive us home through London, naked,' spat Ava. She began to rip his trousers down around his ankles. Paris ripped his white silk shirt off and yanked the sleeves down at the shoulders. They had a considerable amount of trouble removing the collar, but they soon managed to wrench that off his body. Paris and Ava settled into the back seat of the car and cuddled up together. Paris fished a pointed black leather tawse from the picnic basket. She tapped it at the back of their driver's head.

'Now drive, slut! Take us home. We'll decide what to do with you when we get there. You are certainly in a great deal of trouble, that's for sure...' said Ava. She felt a pang of the desire for retribution beginning to form inside her chest.

The car glided out of the car park. Mark felt terrified of the nightmare ride ahead. He felt worried that their journey through London might culminate in his being pulled over by the police. He prayed to himself that there wasn't too much traffic about and hoped that the traffic lights would be merciful. Looking in the rear-view mirror he noticed the glow of Paris and Ava's wicked smiles across their faces. Ava looked squarely into the rear -view mirror and licked her red lips.

WHORE

It was yet another Friday night out in Soho. Kitty looked up and down the busy gothic bar to see if there was anyone interesting mulling about. Throngs of long-haired guys in leather, and mini-skirted goth girls sipped on pints of beer topped with blackcurrant cordial. Pints of Guinness passed over the bar at an alarming rate. Each pint had been finished off with a pentagram drawn in the beer foam on top by the bar staff. Loud metal and punk music blared from black speakers of each corner in the large rowdy pub. Fake spider webs, plastic zombies and horror-themed pinball machines were dotted around different corners of the bar. It was a very riotous type of place. Had there been sawdust on the floor, Kitty thought it would have made a fine location for a rodeo. Outside, black velvet-clad denizens crowded in the small tiled courtyard smoking beside the front door. They chatted amongst themselves, looking tough and unapproachable.

Kitty walked towards a wall that was covered with racks filled with flyers. It showed a selection of neon pink and black flyers advertising rock gigs, metal nights or local fetish clubs. Sifting through the flyers, she couldn't find any events going on that held any appeal. She looked around the bar and decided that after this drink, she would move on to somewhere else.

Having finished her drink, she made her way to the ladies' room. A group of girls hogged the mirror applying heavy black make-up as they gossiped about various men and women from the bar outside. Kitty couldn't be bothered to listen too closely. She just wasn't feeling the vibe of the atmosphere. She hauled her large handbag up onto the sink and began to take off her studded belts and large metal rings. She looked in the mirror. With a few changes, she decided she could easily strip her look back to hit a cocktail bar in the West End. She didn't really know what she was looking for. She felt she just wanted something or someone different today.

Kitty had now stripped her outfit back to a minimum, she now stood admiring her handiwork in the bathroom mirror. She was now wearing just a tight black sleeveless dress, black fishnets, shiny black heels and a with pair of three-quarter-length leather gloves. She brushed her hair, then tied it into a quick chignon bun and walked out of the ladies' room. She headed back towards the wilderness of Soho.

The streets were buzzing. Drunken tourists, groups of lads and hen party girls in pink sashes barged around the streets and bars of the centre of town. None of those types of bars appealed to Kitty very much, as the people that frequented them were invariably an excruciating mixture of drunk and boring. She walked east towards Covent Garden. Covent Garden had a little bit more of an artistic feel to it. As she clicked along the pavement, she could hear music and loud conversations blaring from every bar. The area felt like a war zone composed of a militia made up of the interminably wrecked. She had an inkling that nothing interesting was going to transpire that evening as most of the drunks were too far gone after nine p.m. She lamented to herself about the fact that no matter how attractive or accessible she had made herself look, the chances of finding someone that wasn't too pissed to function was a slim prospect.

Before deciding to ditch out on the West End, she elected to stop for at least one last favourite cocktail in a cellar bar that she liked to occasionally frequent. It was called Freud's. She descended the stairs and quietly chose the last available seat at the bar. She began to peruse the cocktail menu. One of the cocktails stood out amongst the others. It was called a 'Lady-boy'. The description of the cocktail was triple sec, gold tequila and lime juice in a Martini glass, smeared with red lipstick. It sounded like fun. She ordered one from the bartender with her raised black leather-gloved hand, as she waved a twenty-pound note in the air. Kitty looked up and down the bar whilst she waited for her drink. She vaguely glanced up and down the length of the room, trying to see if there was remotely anyone in the slightest bit fuckable in the bar. The congregation was comprised mostly of post-work drinkers and banter merchants in questionably cut suits. They majority of them looked like area managers of some kind. The sight of them was a massive turn-off for Kitty. Not that she would have minded a hot bloke in a suit. But to her, in her current situation, she surmised that the last portion of this evening was destined to be a case of hunting, yet no envisioned quarry to speak of.

Kitty's cocktail arrived. She thanked the bartender and gave him a tip. She lifted the delicate Martini glass to her lips. She smiled to herself. Red lipstick was smeared around the edges of the martini glass. It smudged off the rim and stained her lips. She lifted the glass to her lips a second time. A tall, dirty-blonde haired, blue-eyed stranger spoke in her ear over her shoulder. It startled her a little bit.

'That's an interesting cocktail, what's it called?' he said.

'It's called a "Lady-boy." And what are you called?' she replied.

The man had glint of fascination in his eye.

"I'm called many things, but my name is Karl. Does that mean you like the ladies ... or the boys?' said Karl.

'I am not attracted to a particular sex, I am attracted to types of people,' said Kitty in a flat tone.

'And how would I go about being the right type of person?' said Karl.

Kitty stared at him with a spry, calculating look for a few seconds. She took another sip.

'Well, fortune favours the brave. I like a bit of bravery,' said Kitty mischievously. 'You can start by ordering us both another lady-boy.'

Karl looked at her and grinned. He looked her up and down, the look on his face was very telling that he was trying to figure her out. He raised his hand and called the bartender over.

'Two lady-boys, please,' he said. 'One for the lady, and the other for the boy.'

Kitty smiled at him.

'Thank you,' she said to Karl. Then 'game on,' she thought.

The drinks arrived. Kitty raised her glass and clinked his. She watched as he lifted the glass to his lips. As he drank the cocktail, his lips began to smear with the same red lipstick from the edge of the Martini glass. He looked around the room, smiling boldly, wearing his new lipstick. Kitty laughed.

'That's a good shade on you,' she noted, with a cheeky smile.

'What else have you got?' he said, challenging her.

'Oh! It's like that is it?' she replied. Kitty sifted through her handbag and pulled out a purple eye shadow. Using a single smudge from her index finger, she smeared the colour across his eyes. He looked in the bar mirror.

'That colour suits me,' he said with a spritely smile.

Kitty sent him a beaming grin.

'Now I am just wondering what else you will do after a few drinks,' she said.

'Try me,' he replied. His voice had a slight tone of playful arrogance.

Kitty paused for thought. She knocked back her cocktail.

'Follow me,' she said directly.

Karl followed Kitty. She headed for the ladies' room and dragged him into a cubicle. She then locked the door. To his surprise, she took off her black fishnet stockings and midnight blue suspender belt. She handed them to Karl.

'I dare you to put this on,' she said with a slight giggle, holding out the garments in front of him.

Karl cocked his head sideways. He knew that in London on a Friday night, you could get away with wearing almost anything. But this was a conservative bar. If he walked out into the bar wearing nothing but stockings, suspenders and his boxer shorts. He knew that he would get some very strange looks. At the same point, the buzz of the dare coupled with the knowledge of his relative anonymity in Soho meant that even if people did bat an eyelid, he would never see any of them again.

'What's the worst that could happen?' said Kitty, daring him.

Karl decided to accept her dare. He stripped down in front of her and passed his trousers over to her. He sat down on the closed toilet seat and slid her fishnet stockings on. She fastened the suspender belt around his waist and attached the stockings at their clasps. Karl looked down at his legs. He felt himself getting an instant erection. Kitty put her hand out and drew it along the inside of his thigh.

'That's nice,' she said. 'I like that.'

Kitty grabbed his hand to pull him out of the ladies' room.

'Wooah!' said a startled Karl. 'I am game for going out there, but I don't know if you have noticed but I am going to have to limp out with this raging hard-on.'

'Well I can fix that for you...' said Kitty.

Kitty directed Karl to the edge of the ladies' room sink counter and propped him up against it. Without a word, she yanked his boxers shorts down and began sucking him off. Karl felt an instant rush of relief. His eyes rolled into the back of his head as he listened to the sound and relished the feeling of her wet lips noisily sucking on the head of his cock.

At that moment, a stray bar customer wandered in to the ladies' room. She stopped and stared with a mesmerised look on her face, almost as though she was trying to take in the scene that was going on in front of her. Kitty stopped, looked up and smiled at the girl.

'Can help you?' she said wickedly.

The flustered woman looked at her incredulously.

'Err, no..' she said.

As quickly as the woman had entered the ladies' room, she also vanished out of it.

Kitty returned to sucking Karl's cock. She opened her mouth wide and licked his cock as though she was licking a lollipop. Karl groaned. He could feel himself a few sucks away from cumming. Kitty quickly grabbed the head of his cock and scrunched the end. She could feel the pressure of his cum trying to escape the end of his penis, but it was to no avail. Karl looked down at her with shock.

'You ruined my orgasm!' he exclaimed.

'Only for now,' said Kitty, rubbing her lip with her index finger suggestively. 'You still haven't gone out into the bar with me, but we have solved your raging erection issue. Have we not?

Karl could feel a low, dull aching in his balls. He felt spent, but unsatisfied. It was the strangest sensation. Kitty stood up and looked in the mirror. She began to fish through her handbag, and produced different pots of make-up, which she applied to her face. She picked up a bright red pot of rouge and displayed it in front of Karl.

If you put this blush on and go outside with it on. I'll take you home in a taxi and ride you like a rented mule.

Karl laughed. He knew with a pretty girl in tow, he could certainly get away with just about anything in Central London. He paused for a moment to look at her.

'Okay, then,' he said.

Kitty painted the blush on his cheeks. She let out an unplanned, sadistic giggle. She grabbed his hand and pulled him out into the bar. As they walked back into the bar, several heads turned to look at them. Other women craned their necks upwards with an air of disdain on their faces. A few of the men gave Karl the slyest of grins. Karl and Kitty returned to sit at their two empty bar stools next to the counter.

'May we have two more "lady-boys",' said Kitty to the bartender. Now sporting bare legs, Kitty used her knees to restrain one of Karl's stockinged legs. She began to stroke his leg discreetly. Despite her feigned discretion, she knew everyone in the room was covertly eyeing up them both. It was a wonderfully delicious position to be in, knowing that politeness would halt everyone in the room from making any real comments about them. She reached out with one hand and stroked his leg.

'You feel so sexy now, and you're bold. I find that intriguing and useful.'

'Useful for what?' said Karl.

'Public exhibitionism,' she replied calmly.

'Is that what you are into?' he said.

'That, amongst other things, yes…' said Kitty.

The bartender returned with their drinks. The two clinked glasses and lifted them to their lips, which became increasingly red from the newly smeared lipstick on their third set of martini glasses.

'Let's go,' said Kitty.

'Are we going back to yours?' said Karl.

Kitty lied.

'Yes, we are going there right now,' she replied.

The two got up from the bar stools. There was an undertone of commotion in the room from all the suited barflies and office worker girls, as they watched the shameless duo head for the door.

The woman from the toilet earlier, mumbled at Kitty as she walked past.

'Disgusting,' she said timidly, with a slight tone of aggression.

Kitty turned to her with an evil smile.

'Oh, I promise you, it will be disgusting later,' she retorted. 'Reverse cowgirl and everything, hold on to that image...' she winked.

Karl's eyes brightened with that statement.

'Is it?' he asked Kitty. She didn't answer.

Kitty walked out of the room, holding Karl's hand.

'Come on, Karla. It's sex time!' she said, laughing riotously.

Kitty stood on the grey brick-paved cobbles of the street beside Karl. She did her best to hide him behind her whilst she hailed a taxi. A black cab soon drew up. The electric window on the passenger side slid down.

'Where to?' said the taxi driver.

'Soho, please,' said Kitty. 'We want to go to Brewer Street.'

'So, you live in Soho?' said Karl.

'Err, yes,' yes Kitty. She tired her best not to let her answer sound too cagey.

She looked out of the cab window at the herds of drunks, as the taxi sped the short distance to Soho. The taxi pulled up beside the bright lights, gay bars and neon chaos of central Soho. Kitty handed the taxi driver his fee. They exited the black taxi.

'Wow, this is a terrific location to live in,' said Karl.

'Well, we just need to make a stop first,' said Kitty. 'We need to pick something up.'

Kitty grabbed Karl and pulled him towards the relative privacy behind the blocked-out windows of a seedy looking sex shop.

Inside, the sex shop was littered with mild-mannered looking men browsing the kinky DVD's and sexy magazines. At the far wall, there was a huge rack of sexy clothing and costumes. Kitty walked up to the rack with Karl.

'Now, let's see... What do we like here? Hmm, sexy witch, sexy nurse, sexy pirate! Oh, I like the sexy pirate costume! Do I get a free parrot?' she asked. She lifted the size XL costume off the rack and walked to the counter. She turned to Karl and gave him a deadpan look.

'Want any porn? Want any poppers?' she said.

'Do I need any?' he replied.

'You tell me!' she said.

Karl paid the cashier, who discreetly put the sexy pirate costume in a red and white striped plastic bag. They left the shop. Karl found himself waiting on the pavement beside Kitty, hailing another taxi. A new black cab drew up.

King's Cross, please,' said Kitty to the driver as he lowered the front window of new cab. The two got in.

The taxi sped off towards King's Cross.

Kitty started to unbutton his shirt.

'What are you doing now?' said Karl.

'Put this pirate costume on!' said Kitty seriously.

Karl stared into the front of the cab. The taxi driver seemed conveniently preoccupied watching the road.

'I thought that pirate costume was for you!' he said.

'If you put this pirate costume on, I promise you. I will put on a much better costume when we get back to my place. I've got something that will make your heart jump into your throat. But you must play the game first. Besides, it's turn on for me,' she said.

Karl sighed, then felt a surge of pleasurable danger about this entirely unfamiliar experience. He also noted on how sharp her bargaining skills were at this juncture. He began to put the sexy pirate dress on. Kitty clapped and cheered.

'That's better,' now you are entering the "whore" zone part of your mind. I think that's a much better place for you, don't you?'

By the time Karl had wrangled himself into the pirate dress, the taxi pulled up behind King's Cross station. Karl paid the taxi this time.

The two exited and walked towards the dark archways at the bottom of the station. Random people mulled around the station, smoking cigarettes and ambling in the streets.

With an eagle-like stare, Kitty began to scope out the people that were hanging around. Her eyes scanned the vista, looking for the most conspicuous men.

A young reasonably attractive road worker sidled up quietly to them, winked, and then walked on. Kitty turned.

'He's on. Do you like him?' she said.

'What? Do you?' replied Karl. 'What are we doing?'

Kitty whistled at the man. He turned, acknowledged them then walked back towards them. Kitty addressed the man.

'Meet us in the park in five minutes,' she said.

The man nodded, and headed straight towards the park.

Karl felt a moment of disbelief.

'Are you a hooker?' said Karl.

Kitty laughed.

'Not at all! But with that said, what have you got against hookers?' she exclaimed.

'Nothing,' said Karl.

'Well, good. Because before we go, you are about to become one.'

'How is that going to work?' he said with a face of shock.

'Listen, don't worry about it. What you do will turn me on ridiculously. What have you got to lose?' she repeated. There was something wild about Kitty that made Karl want to go along with her scheme. Up to this point, it seemed that almost everything she enjoyed, involved a level of anonymity. It was as though she was taking advantage of the faceless throngs of strangers in the London horde. It was refreshingly liberating. He was fascinated to find out what she got up to. He started to feel himself being sucked in to wanting to discover what she would make happen next.

Karl was also bemused enough by this new experience to give himself over to the situation. He knew he indeed had nothing to lose by following her. He knew, that in London, being dressed as he was would make the public assume that he probably just another partying drunk out for the night. The London consciousness had a way of drawing its' own conclusions and making rational explanations for the sights it saw. He barely knew this girl, and yet he suddenly found himself in a situation where whatever he was about to do next would be completely anonymous, if that's what he wanted. He felt an incredible rush of new freedom with Kitty. He decided these fresh circumstances were not something worth any further questioning. He resolved to follow her, and find out what was going to happen next. Also, he felt more plausible wearing a pirate costume dress by walking beside a sexy girl, rather than walking away on his own.

Kitty squeezed his hand. She led him up the dark backstreets and traffic to the small park behind King's Cross station. They spied the workman that they had arranged to meet. He stood furtively by the entrance, smoking a cigarette. He inhaled his cigarette deeply. He spoke through the smoke in an East End accent.

'Alright?' said the workmen, in his fast London dialect.

'Up for some fun?' said Kitty.

'God, you're fast!' said Karl.

'No rules here, pirate girl,' said Kitty. 'We all do what we like round this manor.'

'You've done this before?' said Karl.

Kitty didn't answer him. She shot him a sneaky wink. She walked over to the workman and began to whisper in his ear. They stepped a few feet away for a minute and began to talk in hushed tones as they looked back at Karl. The workman glanced over towards Karl and nodded to Kitty. He handed a small, round metal object to her. Kitty gave the workman a very sly smile. Kitty and the workman returned to Karl.

'Let's go,' she said. 'I know where there's a picnic table nearby. It's quiet there.'

Still not sure of what was about to happen, Karl followed them into the deserted park. The street lights progressively thinned out, until there was just a few light sources dotted around nearby.

The three stopped at the dimly lit picnic table. Kitty addressed the stranger.

My name's Emily, and this is my whore. I call her Cindy. Cindy is going to suck your cock.

'Oh no, I'm not!' said Karl.

The man unzipped his flies to reveal his flaccid cock.

'Fine,' said Kitty. 'More cock for me.'

Kitty leant over the man who perched himself on the picnic table. Kitty began to lick and suck on his prick. She turned and gave Karl a hungry look.

'Tastes good, Cindy...' she said devilishly. 'This is your chance ... No one's ever going to know ...'

Karl watched as the man arched his back with pleasure. What she said was true, Karl thought. No one *was* ever going to know. And the moment felt deeply dreamy and mesmerising. He knew that whatever he chose to do at this point was completely without recourse. This chance to join in and find out what it really felt like to suck a stranger's cock, meant freedom from anyone ever having the knowledge of his actions. He edged over to the couple and gingerly rubbed his hand over the man's chest. The man grabbed his hand and moved it down onto his prick. Karl began to rub it, feeling an incredible sense of liberation. The man gently urged Karl to suck him.

'Suck it,' he said. 'My cum tastes good.'

Kitty tuned to kiss Karl on his neck. She reached down and began to stroke his raging hard-on through the skirt of his party dress. The man reached down and stroked Karl's head as he sucked.

'That's it,' said Kitty. 'Suck it, you little bitch. You like that cock in your mouth, don't you? That's because you are a dirty whore. I knew it the first minute I saw you.'

Karl focussed on sucking the man's cock. He could feel the force of the man cum. He grabbed Karl's head and began to thrust his close-to-orgasm cock in and out of his mouth rapidly. Kitty bent down and began to wank Karl off at the same time. Kitty spied out of the corner of her eye that they were not entirely alone. She noticed another stranger appear at the edge of the clearing by the picnic table. She acknowledged him briefly. He approached them and began wanking furiously at the site of Karl sucking the workman's cock. Kitty grabbed the strangers hand and shoved it down her dress. He seemed a bit taken aback by her actions, but decided to start fondling and grabbing at her tits with one hand, whilst heavily masturbating with the other.

Kitty sighed. She could feel the air against her face and looked up at the distant streetlights. She spied another couple of guys watching silently from behind a treeline. They were wanking themselves off and watching them intently. To Kitty, this animal state of mind seemed a thousand miles away from the nearby bustle of King's Cross station. It was fascinating to her how swiftly that a simple patch of isolated ground and several anonymous figures could reconnect the animal side of her being again. The dressing up, the taxis, the transactions and meetings were all just a set of rituals and vehicles that led up to this state-of-mind. It had been what she was craving all along. Those few moments of being disconnected from the pretensions of day-to-day existence, and a few minutes of animal sex would be enough to get her through the insanity of all the social niceties and behaviours that made London society so interminably boring, and so infinitely stressful. These moments always helped her to escape that. There was no other way to explain it. She grabbed the workmen's cock out of Karl's mouth and began to rub on it violently. She turned to Karl and kissed him hungrily, ramming her tongue up inside of his mouth. She could feel the pressure from the workman's cock beginning to react. Her hand became covered with sticky white globules of cum. The workman settled back on the picnic table, looking post orgasmic. He lit up a cigarette. Kitty grabbed the head of Karl's cock and squeezed it hard for a second time. He howled. She smiled.

'Not again!' said Karl. 'You are trying to ruin my orgasm again! I can't believe you!'

'You're not getting an orgasm until you go back to my place,' she said. Her face was adorable and sinister all at the same time. She displayed the most affectionately deviant smile towards Karl.

The workman sat up.

'I think I blacked out a little bit for a minute,' he said with a bewildered look.

'Well, we aim to please,' said Kitty. 'Come on Cindy, let's go get you sorted out.'

'I could have been sorted out twice, by now,' he said with a little sigh.

'Yeah, but that would have been only temporary gratification. It would have been empty and hollow. What's fun about that?' replied Kitty. She turned around to the workman. Licking the cum off her hand, she graciously shook his.

'Nice to meet you,' she said plainly. 'Time to go Cindy. You are coming home with me now! Come on.'

Kitty grabbed his hand and he began to straighten himself up for the walk back to the station cab rank.

'So,' said Kitty. 'How are you feeling?'

'Strangely exhilarated… and frustrated,' said Karl.

'The frustration is going to come to an end. If you really want it to. It will be a distant memory soon.'

Karl felt perplexed by her cryptic reply. He didn't have anything to add, so they walked on. He realised that although she seemed intent on leading the events of the evening, he really knew very little about her. There was something addictive about the dark look of her and the way she carried herself that made him feel more mentally free, but also quite safe. He couldn't explain it to himself, but he felt a sense that he knew he could trust her judgement. It seemed to him that she knew what she was doing. She had this aura of always having something pre-planned. Kitty had opened a door for him with her streetwise understanding of the inner workings of an underground part of London. He never even knew that part existed before. The fleeting thought enthralled him. He surmised that there must be a lot of other things that she must have known. She was certainly very difficult to second guess. He found it a little hard to fully understand why she seemed so bent on doing something other than just picking him up and taking him home for straight sex. That was originally what he had been expecting from her in that bar. And yet, he could feel his mind beginning to stretch from being in her presence. In the minimal amount of time that he had known her, he had found himself quickly adopting circumstances which he would never have previously agreed to. Now, he found himself wanting more.

Kitty and Karl arrived at the taxi rank.

'Where can I take you?' said the cab driver.

'Islington,' said Kitty. 'Coronet Street.'

'Very well, get in,' said the taxi driver.

The taxi sped up the road towards Islington. Karl fell silent as he tried to take in recent events. His mind felt as though it had shifted to another dimension. He started to wonder if any part of this night was real.

Kitty looked out of the window, now completely disaffected. She clocked Karl's starry-eyed look. The taxi pulled up into Coronet street. The got out. Kitty lit up a cigarette. She walked Karl to her front door and fished her flat keys out of her pocket. They entered the front door. Hanging in the vestibule was a rack of typical hallway implements: umbrellas, coat hangers and bags, along with a dog lead and collar. Kitty lifted the collar and fastened it around Karl's neck. He raised an eyebrow, but let her continue.

'You didn't think I was going to let you run loose in the house without a lead, did you? You would be peeing all over the place, like an over-excitable puppy in new surroundings.'

'I wasn't planning on peeing all over the place,' replied Karl.

'Well, I'm not taking any chances,' she huffed. 'The last time I let one of you naughty little scamps in my house without a lead, half of my underwear went missing.'

Kitty clipped the dog leash onto the collar around Karl's neck and tugged him into the house.

'Let's get changed into something else,' said Kitty.

She towed Karl up the stairs by his lead and stopped facing her vast wardrobe. She leafed through the huge rail of garments and produced a pink latex maid's uniform. She then chose a black chain mail dress for herself. In front of Karl, she began to peel off her clothes and step into the dress.

'Help me fasten it,' she said to Karl. He stared transfixed by her curvaceous, olive-skinned body.

He found the clasp of the dress and fastened it around her neck. Kitty, now satisfied with her outfit and the fact that it looked like it was hanging correctly, held the pink latex maid's uniform out to Karl.

'I want you to wear this for me,' she said. 'It would turn me on immensely.'

It felt like déjà vu. Something in the flat, matter-of-fact, childishly demanding tone of her voice made her directives impossible to resist. He put on the latex dress and noted the strange tightness of it against his body. Kitty produced a long red wig from the cupboard and fitted it to his scalp with a hair pin. She began to play with the shape of the tresses. Then, having decided that it looked correct, she repainted his lips and eyes with a make-up palette that had been resting on a nearby dressing table.

'A famous model's Mum once said that "You should be a maid in the living room, a cook in the kitchen, and a whore in the bedroom." But as far as I am concerned, you should be a whore everywhere. That makes a great deal more sense to me. And you, are.'

'For the rest of our time together, I am going to now call you Cindy. And I want you to call me Maîtresse,' said Kitty sternly.

'What does Maîtresse mean?' said Karl / Cindy.

'It's French, for... teacher. Now come with me, all that covert activity out in the dark has made me too chilly. You will have to give me a bath, to heat me up again,' she said.

'Dressed like this?' said Cindy. 'I thought me dressing like this was going to turn you on.'

'It has,' replied Kitty. 'But I need a bath first. You must wash me. You don't need to assume that I am planning to stay clean for all that long afterwards.'

Kitty led her newly dressed, painted, pink latex maid up to the bathroom by her dog lead. It was a large room with a claw-footed white bathtub in the centre. She stood back and looked at Cindy, folding her arms.

'I would like you to draw my bath in a delicate, ladylike fashion, Cindy. There is bubble bath in the pink glass bottle. I like my baths hot.' Kitty's voice a slightly bratty, spoiled tone.

Cindy took her first orders in as accommodating a fashion as she could. She turned the tap on the bath and put the plug in, then lifted the bubble bath bottle from a washstand to pour it under the running tap. Kitty unclipped her chain mail dress. It dropped to the floor. She stood before Cindy, now completely naked. She put out her hand. Cindy took it, his face formed a little look of confusion. Kitty ignored his confusion by stepping onto a single wooden step, then descending into the bathtub. The water and bubbles began to fill up all around Kitty. The sight of her beautiful naked body and large breasts made Karl long for her. He wondered what finally taking her would feel like. That thought brought a sense of impropriety to his mind. He found himself entertaining a flash of thought that she may in fact, be too good for him. He felt there was a hierarchy forming, where she was the boss and he was the servant. It filled him with a strange, unreal type of thrill.

Kitty sighed with relaxation. The room was now very steamed up to the point of forming hot clouds. She admired her latex maid as she waited patiently for her next command. Kitty picked up a bath sponge.

'Wash me,' said Kitty. 'But do it gently.'

Cindy rubbed dome soap into the sponge and caressed it across Kitty's back. He watched hypnotically as the soap slip down Kitty's beautiful neck. He went on to glide the sponge up and down the length of Kitty's smooth legs. Kitty grabbed his hand and put it under the water. She guided his hand towards her pussy.

'Wash me there,' said Kitty.

Cindy began to gently rub Kitty's clitoris in slow, circular motions. She arched her back with pleasure, forcing her tits above the waterline.

'Lick me,' she said. Kitty raised her pussy up out of the water and held on to a rail behind the bath.

Cindy obliged dutifully. Cindy could feel new beads of pre-cum beginning to drip from the end of her cock. Kitty looked down and noticed the hardness of Cindy's penis straining under the latex.

'I bet you would like to put your cock inside of me right now, wouldn't you?' said Kitty.

'Oh yes,' said Cindy. 'Yes, I would give anything.'

'Anything?' said Kitty. She was now writhing with pleasure as she watched the maid lick.

'Yes, anything,' said Cindy.

'Get in the bath with me,' said Kitty.

Cindy began to take her dress off.

'No get in the bath with me as you are,' demanded Kitty.

The shiny, wet pink latex glistened under the light. Kitty began to rub the fabric with glee. It squeaked a lot. Kitty showed a concerted interest in rubbing the bulge where Cindy's erection strained against the dress.

'You feel exquisite to me,' said Kitty. 'Stay there. I will be back in a minute.' Kitty, still naked, got up from the bath and left the room briefly. She returned wearing a large, purple strap on cock.'

She edged herself up to the bath beside and Cindy.

'I want you to suck my cock, like the dirty whore you know you are. Did you know, that I sold your mouth to that workman earlier for one-pound sterling? As far as I am concerned, that makes you truly a cheap whore. Four hours ago, you were a lad scamming on random girls. But now, your name is Cindy and we both know you are a slut maid for hire to the lowest bidder. I find that extremely hot, knowing what you really are.'

Kitty walked to the edge of the bath and pushed the purple dildo towards Cindy's mouth. Cindy tried to lightly kiss it at first, but soon felt the strength of it as it slid past her lips. Cindy looked up, watching transfixed as the naked Kitty forced the purple strap-on into her mouth. Cindy began to suck.

'I am glad you made that nice and clean, my little bitch.' Kitty grabbed Cindy by her wet collar and lead. She pulled her out of the bath.

'Bend over the bath,' she ordered.

Nervously, Cindy lowered herself to her knees. She stared straight ahead. It now felt completely impossible to not comply with whatever Kitty asked of her. Every new moment had a way of unveiling further alien pleasures. Kitty rolled the latex of the pink maid's dress up over Cindy's hips. She pulled Cindy's ass cheeks apart and spat into her ass hole. She straightened Cindy's back and pushed the head of the purple strap-on the first few inches inside of Cindy's ass. It felt ticklish to Cindy, but she could also feel herself wanting Kitty to push it in further.

'Don't move,' said Kitty. 'We have to wait for your muscles to relax first. Otherwise you will be in the wrong sort of agony. That's not what we want. Trust me.'

Cindy waited patiently. Her cock stiffened as she felt the head of the strap-on push its' way further in.

Cindy felt her ass muscles finally relax. Then she felt a tremendous urge to push back on Kitty's strap-on. It was the most incredible sensation. Kitty reached under Cindy and began to play with Cindy's cock.

'That's it. Good girl. You're being a good girl for Kitty, aren't you? Tell me everything that happened to you today whilst I fuck your ass.'

Cindy panted.

'You, you sucked my cock in a bar... then, you dressed me up as a slutty girl in Soho. Then ... you took me to King's Cross and made me suck the cock of a stranger for twenty pence and I felt cheap afterwards. Now... now you're fucking me up my ass and I am dressed as a pink latex maid....' Cindy's cock felt ready to explode with showers of thick cum, as he recited the recent events.

Kitty cooed. She thrusted the dildo into Cindy's ass.

'That's because underneath it all, you know that you really are a just a whore. And if you can keep that up in this town, you will go very far.'

END

Printed in Great Britain
by Amazon

29024448R00086